Echoing ing Reality

에코잉 리얼리티

Echoing Reality

초판 1쇄 인쇄	2014년 05월 26일
초판 1쇄 발행	2014년 06월 02일

지은이　　김 한 빈
펴낸이　　손 형 국
펴낸곳　　(주)북랩
편집인　　선일영　　　　　　　　편집　　이소현, 이윤채, 조민수
디자인　　이현수, 신혜림, 김루리　　제작　　박기성, 황동현, 구성우
마케팅　　김회란

출판등록　2004. 12. 1(제2012-000051호)
주소　　　서울시 금천구 가산디지털 1로 168, 우림라이온스밸리 B동 B113, 114호
홈페이지　www.book.co.kr
전화번호　(02)2026-5777　　　　　　팩스　　(02)2026-5747

ISBN　　979-11-5585-235-4 03810 (종이책)　979-11-5585-236-1 05810 (전자책)

이 도서의 국립중앙도서관 출판시도서목록(CIP)은 서지정보유통지원시스템 홈페이지(http://seoji.nl.go.kr)와
국가자료공동목록시스템(http://www.nl.go.kr/kolisnet)에서 이용하실 수 있습니다.
(CIP제어번호 : 2014016641)

Echoing Reality

에코잉 리얼리티

Reality

김한빈 지음

book Lab

Word of Recommendation

I still remember the day Han Bin sat in my office asking about taking various English classes. I asked her why she wanted to take more than one English class and also be a student aid for an English class.

Her answer was, "I love to read and analyze books. I love English classes and I want to learn more." I thought, "Really?" Later, half jokingly, I asked, "Why not publish your own book some day?" Her response was, "I would like to and I have already written a lot." I couldn't believe her drive and passion to share her love for reading. It has been a year since I met her for the first time and I have seen nothing but a genuine love for reading.

I would highly recommend young people to read Han Bin's book. It's full of passion for literature and excitement for reading. Han Bin has analyzed and written her thoughts about many wonderful works from the past. My hope is that this book can be a little spark that can set a huge fire in the hearts of teenagers where the riches of knowledge from books are being replaced by digital games and gadgets.

God Bless,

Nitta Song

High School Principal
International School of Qingdao

Foreword

I have always loved to read. Starting from when I was very young, books were my constant companions, my perpetual friends. Everywhere I went I would leave behind me a little hurricane of books that I never remembered to clean up; my mother often had to remind me to organize the mess, but even so I sometimes forgot. On one such occasion my mother banned me from reading books the entire next day and I spent it perched miserably in front of the TV. The habit of reading voraciously has remained with me throughout my life. Of course when I was young I was strongly inclined to fantasy, and as I grew older I learned to love the books that empathized with the new sights I was seeing, but on the whole I was as indiscriminate as I was insatiable. I loved everything regardless of genre or era as long as it gave me pleasure.

But until I entered high school I was somewhat of a lopsided reader, since it wasn't until that point I realized what books could really mean. My high school offered literature and composition courses in the afternoons, after the intensive Korean classes of the daytime. These classes had a cathartic effect on me. They also opened my eyes to a whole new world. For the first time, literature gained purpose and social meaning: it was no more merely the pleasurable device that I had taken it to be.

I suppose I had realized it, if unconsciously, from before. When I had opportunities to share my English with students who were struggling more than most, they forged friendships with me and brought parts of their lives into mine. Those brief glimpses into the lives they lived left me with a thirst and a love for books relating the pain that these students themselves were too mature and controlled to show me. But until high school I took those books only as methods of empathy, never as actual vehicles of powerful messages that could incite changes in the society. To a degree, the realization was intoxicating. Analysis of literary works became a constant and startlingly crisp joy. Empathy no longer ended in mere empathy but broadened into a call asking for the awareness and recognition of pain.

If I hadn't come to China, I doubt my love of literature would have resulted in anything quite so tangible as this book. It was the first time the weaknesses of the socially neglected had struck so deep in me, because it was the first time the weaknesses were so vulnerable and so manifest- firstly, in the various stages of leprosy that plagued some of these people; and secondly, in the lack of governmental support that was by all rights theirs. Here, in wayward towns and houses buried deep in mountain slopes, I met various members of the afflicted elderly, and in the ways they interacted with me I read their painful stories of ostracization and humility. During the brief silent moments their knobbly stumps clasped my complete hands, I heard, almost as clearly as if it had been said, that to keep silent was to indulge in cowardice. The plight of these people had to be told, in one way or another; their message of neglect and pain had to be communicated.

And there were other things, too, that I decided I wanted to tell-the friends that I made from some of the most impoverished villages, what I had seen in them and with them. The things I had seen in my high school life and in my middle school life that left strong enough of an impact on me and impressed me in certain ways to change.

This book is far from being a complete analysis of the faults that can be seen in today's society, but it strikes as close as it can get to an analysis of some of the faults that a seventeen-year-old can see, and some that only a seventeen-year-old could see, being in immediate contact with her surroundings. But it necessarily has the limitations of an adolescent viewer and I beg the reader to be lenient with the overhasty generalizations and immature judgments that are bound to appear.

I want to thank my classmates and friends, who shared with me the many precious memories that inspired me to write. Especial thanks goes to Sandra and Joon, who often kept me company in my love for literary analysis, and my high school teachers in Korea, who taught me worlds in literature. My favorite ISQ teachers, Ms. Blanks and Ms. Thompson, thank you so much for showing me such overwhelming patience and love and care, even during the months when you were insanely busy; and Mrs. Song, thank you so much and more, for planting this idea in my head in the first place! And most of all, thanks to my family- Dad, Mom, my sister Soo Bin, and my Aunt Vivian- who all coaxed me through the bad times and loved me through the good times and helped me to believe that a seventeen-year-old's opinion actually might go heard.

Especial thanks goes to BookLab, who spent long hours in helping my work become published print.

For the reader there is just one last note: when I was very young one of my favorite books was *Little Lord Fauntleroy*. To be sure I never thought there was much else to it except for the innocence of a young boy transforming his crabby grandfather. Very recently I thought about it again and concluded that it was rather like a mild propaganda of noblesse oblige. But whatever it is, the importance of a sentence Mrs. Errol says does not change. For in her wise words is the very reason that all writers write, and the reason I tried to become one:

"And that is best of all, Ceddie, -it is better than everything else, that the world should be a little better because a man has lived- even ever so little better, dearest."

— Mrs. Errol, Little Lord Fauntleroy

Word of Recommendation   *004*

Foreword   *006*

Life on Paper- Novels | Part One

The Great Gatsby, **by Scott F. Fitzgerald**   *016*

Tender is the Night, **by Scott F. Fitzgerald**   *025*

A Rose for Emily, **by William Faulkner**   *036*

Their Eyes Were Watching God, **by Zora Neale Hurston**   *043*

Beloved, **by Toni Morrison**   *053*

Through the Looking-Glass, **by Lewis Carroll**   *059*

Atlas Shrugged & The Fountainhead, **by Ayn Rand**   *069*

The Adventures of Huckleberry Finn, **by Mark Twain**   *080*

Roman Fever, **by Edith Wharton**   *089*

The Age of Innocence, **by Edith Wharton**   *098*

Part Two *Life on Stage- Plays*

108   The Importance of Being Earnest, by Oscar Wilde

118   An Ideal Husband, by Oscar Wilde

127   Lady Windermere's Fan & A Woman of No Importance, by Oscar Wilde

136   Mrs. Warren's Profession & Pygmalion, by George Bernard Shaw

149   A Doll's House, by Henrik Ibsen

160   Hedda Gabler, by Henrik Ibsen

170   A Streetcar Named Desire, by Tennessee Williams

181   Cat on a Hot Tin Roof, by Tennessee Williams

191   Macbeth, by Shakespeare

Life in Life

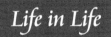

Part Three

The Glass Menagerie, by Tennessee Williams   *202*

The Pearl, by John Steinbeck   *213*

Frankenstein, by Mary Shelley   *225*

Works Referenced   *251*

Echoing
Reality

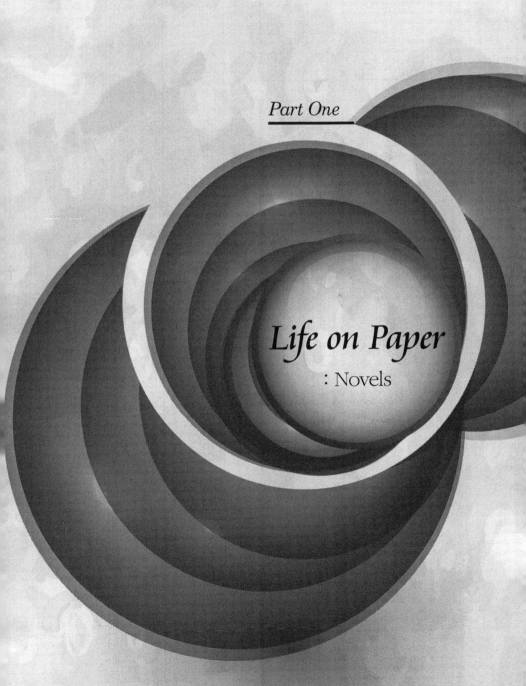

Part One

Life on Paper

: Novels

The Great Gatsby

Introduction

I think I was in seventh grade when I first read *The Great Gatsby*. It was one of those forbidden books that I read on the sly. I often did that, unbeknownst to my parents- I first read *To Kill a Mockingbird* when I was in third grade. But unlike Harper Lee's timeless classic, which I had been unable to understand until I was in fifth grade, I was able to understand *Gatsby* straight away. And from the very beginning, I fell in love with the book.

At first I didn't know why I liked *Gatsby* so much. Then I thought I had fallen in love with the very wealth of the surroundings. When I was young I took a childish pleasure in reading lengthy descriptions of food or scenery, and reading *Gatsby* was like grasping at the memory of those precious times.

And then after that, of course, I thought I had fallen in love with Jay Gatsby himself. There is some captivating force of mystery about Gatsby, though the mystery is incomplete. The narrator, Nick, is able to see through the gaps in the lies that Gatsby spins about himself, and he is careful to tell the reader of all his observations. The way that Gatsby starts talking about himself, only to get tangled in one of his lies and fall back on the truth, was reminiscent of the way I had gone about my own childhood falsehoods. We all love best the characters that we can empathize with.

It took me a long time to realize that I had fallen in love with the author behind the book- or rather, his skill with words. There was a certain sublimity to the phrases that he concocted, the words that were scientifically mixed to create a deliberate amount of half-dreamy conceit and cockiness. Fitzgerald taught me the full impact that words, wrought carefully, could have.

I first realized it when I was mouthing the title to myself. It was interesting, I mused. The use of hard 'g' after hard 'g' forces the reader to keep her mouth pulled back as she reads it, so that she pronounces the word harshly- almost as if out of contempt. The title was so fun to read that I kept on mouthing it. The beauty of the phrases struck after that.

Till today *The Great Gatsby* remains one of my favorite works. For me it seems to be one of those works that are admirable, if for nothing else, then at least for the beauty of the pure genius behind the words.

The Really Truly Great Gatsby

"Some books should be tasted, some devoured, but only a few should be chewed and digested thoroughly."

- Sir Francis Bacon

I've always liked to skim books. I don't really know why. Ever since I was very young, it was just about a habit to rush through one book as quickly as possible and move onto the next.

Mr. Keating, my high school Literature teacher, told me once that it was my fundamental curiosity.

"You're as curious as a mouse when it comes to these things," he said. "You sniff the pages- whisk through them- your eyes sparkle and your little paws shuffle through like a blur of a whirlwind. And then when you find that bit of cheese you're looking for you snatch it up and devour it with your eyes before you start chomping."

I was always proud of being a fast reader, and it definitely had its benefits. Being a fast reader meant that I never had to worry about not being able to do my reading homework. During the summer session Mr. Henderson set us to read seven chapters of *The Catcher in the Rye* per day. By itself it wouldn't have been too much of a struggle for any student, but Ms. Lowett always had some type of composition assignment ready every day. Seha told me on the third day that he had barely caught two hours of sleep the night before and asked me if I had finished the day's reading assignment.

"I finished the book the day I bought it," I said.

Seha looked at me as if I was a freak.

Perhaps I was. At any rate, being known as this type of freak was something that was actually pretty enjoyable. But it had its drawbacks, too. I recall confiding to Selena that every time I re-read a book, I would find a treasure in it that I hadn't been able to find the first time. This meant that I generally would have to read through a book three or four times before I had seen and thought through everything considered important. And if a book wasn't considered interesting enough the first time for me to reinvestigate, then that became a book whose full impact was forever lost to me.

But knowing this didn't inspire me to give this habit up. It was much too fun and much too habitual. So I continued to skip and skim, whipping across like a little engine at full steam, sorting books into ever-growing piles labeled Good and Bad- as far as could be sorted from a freshman's perspective.

That is, until I re-read *The Great Gatsby*, a treasure of a book I had read and loved in seventh grade, but had left discarded since then.

The most captivating part about *The Great Gatsby* is the superb language with which it is written. It is the type of book that, as

Bacon says, must be chewed and digested thoroughly, but only after it has been sufficiently tasted and devoured. Skimming does not work with this book. To fully grasp the startling and wonderful sublimity and aptness of the words that Fitzgerald uses, the book must be read slowly, each of the phrases lingering in the mind like the echo of a song.

When discussing the Jazz Age, there are two parts that necessarily must be communicated in order to discuss it properly: its opulence and its mechanicalness. Fitzgerald, with the sheer power of his words, deftly condenses all the social implications of the era into these two aspects.

Since Fitzgerald's use of language is the defining characteristic of *The Great Gatsby*, it will be easiest to inspect the book through its quotes.

The suggestiveness of the opulence in Fitzgerald's masterpiece can be most clearly seen through the way he describes Gatsby's lifestyle: "There was a machine in the kitchen which could extract the juice of two hundred oranges in half an hour if a little button was pressed two hundred times by a butler's thumb." (Fitzgerald, 26) At this point the reader is already aware of the fact that five crates of oranges and lemons come from New York to the West Egg every weekend for the sake of parties. By stressing the fact that the machine is the one that extracts the juice, and undermining the role of the butler in making it, the wealth in Gatsby's house seems aggrandized. No more is there the need for human labor, which is more often than not failing and unstable. Machines, as expensive as they might be, are all that are necessary.

In tandem with the opulence this quote flaunts, is also the aspect of artificiality. Human interaction has ceased to have its importance. The butler is bypassed in favor of the machine. The button is what stimulates the machine to extract the juice; the butler's thumb is the only part of the butler that is necessary. Although the world of the desensitized high-class is not necessarily a part of life that Gatsby longs for, his goal of pursuit- Daisy- is the very embodiment of the high-class life, and his own lifestyle necessarily comes to imitate theirs.

Fitzgerald uses music exceptionally effectively in order to convey different atmospheres and different scenes. When Gatsby describes what he first sees in Daisy he explains that her "artificial world was redolent of orchids and pleasant, cheerful snobbery and orchestras which set the rhythm of the year, summing up the sadness and suggestiveness of life in new tunes" (Fitzgerald, 96). This quote shows the extent of the frivolity ruling in Daisy's life. If her world can be so comprehensively defined by music, then it is at best a shallow and stylized representation of life. Thus the extent of what Daisy feels in her life can only be a shadow, an imitation of real emotions. A world contained within such a narrow spectrum of emotion and depth cannot produce anything but the shallowest type of artificiality.

In a way this, again, highlights the hypocrisy of the Jazz Age world: the life of the socially elite finds less truth in existence than the life of the very poor. If at least the lives of the destitute feel the truth in the pain of poverty, then the rich are able to completely ignore the truth, enclosing themselves within a cage of tinkling melodies that they call life.

With all this artificiality, hypocrisy, and meaningless opulence surrounding us, the main character himself comes as a relief, a brief interlude showing in a flash all that is good in humanity. Fitzgerald uses the following words to describe Gatsby's smile: "It was one of those rare smiles with a quality of eternal reassurance in it ⋯ It understood you just so far as you wanted to be understood, believed in you as you would like to believe in yourself, and assured you that it had precisely the impression of you that, at your best, you hoped to convey." (Fitzgerald, 32) Gatsby's smile, a symbol of everything that is good and real and comforting in a showy world of swirling false emotions, shows Fitzgerald's contempt for the high-bred society of the Jazz Age. Gatsby narrowly escapes being ridiculous as he tries to emulate the elite class of his time, but nonetheless the warmth that he has is universally felt and draws everyone, invited or uninvited, within his circle. By showing the charm of the man underlying the rumors and the extravagant waste and his ostracization, Fitzgerald turns the sympathies against the rich East Eggers, in a subtle but swift stroke.

The only quote that remains to be analyzed, then, is the last quote, possibly the most famous out of all of Fitzgerald's works: "So we beat on, boats against the current, borne back ceaselessly into the past." (Fitzgerald, 115) Fourteen pithy words summarize the entire spectacular decadence in Fitzgerald's masterpiece. It is hard not to love Fitzgerald for such a sentence. As difficult as it is for man to escape his past, he is necessarily swept back into it even as he tries to escape from its clutches. The frivolous artificiality of the Jazz Age, in particular, is so shallow as to be excruciatingly painful, chafing our skin continuously, as it grasps us and refuses to let us go from its swamping grasp. This sentence, then, is an oath that swears remembrance of the painful opulence of the Jazz Age. It swears that the past will never be forgotten, although it is so painful as for people to long to be liberated from it.

Often there are books that have survived the ages but seem to have received the laudatory praises of the past without having deserved them. *The Great Gatsby* is a spectacular work that truly deserves all the praises from the past that it has received- and indeed, it deserves those of the future as well. For is this book not, in essence, a book swearing eternal allegiance on remembering and avoiding the clutches of the past? The Great Gatsby is indeed as great as its name claims to be.

Tender is the Night

Introduction

"Again. Fitzgerald. Again?"

Selena sniffed, eyeing the book I was carrying to the cafeteria. I bristled slightly.

"Listen to the pot calling the kettle black. Have you forgotten May 1st?"

She laughed. Selena was infatuated with DiCaprio, and from the moment she had known that he would be acting Jay Gatsby in the 2013 version of *The Great Gatsby*, conversations with her somehow turned to Gatsby or Fitzgerald, one way or another. We had been discussing it since the beginning of the year- on the sly during P.E., at lunch, in whispers during study hall, at dinner, in Literature class- but even after two months we still hadn't finished analyzing Daisy or Jordan for all the literary worth in that book. And we both enjoyed it.

But in all fairness, this was the third Fitzgerald book Selena had seen me carrying around, and the second time she had seen me carrying around this particular book. It wasn't because I was in love with DiCaprio; I had the sense not to say this to her face, but she knew it all the same. She knew that I talked about *The Great Gatsby* as much as she did because I admired Fitzgerald, and she also knew that I wasn't planning to watch the movie. Selena knew a lot about me, but she tolerated more.

"Is it good, anyhow?" she asked.

"Very. It's classic Fitzgeraldian. Not as good as *Gatsby*, though."

She wrinkled her nose. "That's a disappointment."

"Mmm. But the leading guys are similar."

Selena half turned towards me as she grabbed her lunch tray.

"Really? Is it, you know, same old, or a different plot?"

"Oh, different. And hey, at least it's got a plot." I said as I rolled my eyes, and she snickered, remembering how I had complained to her as I struggled through *The Beautiful and Damned.*

"Well, it's Fitzgerald, after all. His stories are glorified anecdotes."

Glorified anecdotes. The phrase clung to us during lunch and into the afternoon, as I started reading *Tender is the Night.* Every once in a while, as I flipped a page, I would see Selena blinking owlishly behind her black-rimmed Prada glasses as she did when she was pleased with something she had thought up of. Glorified anecdotes-yes, she was right.

But anecdotes, despise what they may suggest, are hardly ever told without purpose. Even if it is just to pass the time, anecdotes have reason for being told. And so it was with Fitzgerald's book: although the book seems like nothing more than a sequence of sketches tracing the spectacular demise of a likable character, Fitzgerald had a definite message in mind when he related it to us.

The real fun of the book, then, lies in trying to determine what Fitzgerald was trying to say, listening to the soft whisper of the pages as they swish by with the hours. Just what does this lengthy glorified anecdote tell us?

Juxtaposition in a Work of Social Criticism: Tender is the Night

Tender is the Night is undeniably a tragedy, a literary work delineating the life of a hero from his perigee to his apogee. But more than that, it functions as an implicit critique on social decadence- more exactly, the ostentation of the Roaring Twenties, the latter half of which the book takes as its setting- and the sparkle of sensitivity only endowed on such works is scintillating and alive in *Tender*.

The demise of the hero, then, is forced to retreat into the background, the raw pain of his failure disguised in a gentle and elegant hand while the author turns his full attention to the critique. To communicate the tragedy of the piece, the author must necessarily turn to subtler techniques and gentler methods so that they will touch the reader's subconscious without detracting attention from the conscious. In *The Great Gatsby*, Fitzgerald manipulated syntax, using elegant to fragmented sentences in order to convey the change in emotions as well as the explicit profligacy of the Jazz Age. But in *Tender is the Night* he experiments with a more contextual device, the juxtaposition of acting and reality, which highlights the rise and fall of characters and simultaneously gives depth to the plot by providing manifold layers on which the story can unfold. The three main characters of the book are Rosemary Hoyt, Dick Diver, and Nicole Diver, and they all display this juxtaposition in their personalities, though to differing degrees.

In the beginning of the book, ironically, the least experienced "actor" is the only one pursuing a real acting career: starlet Rosemary Hoyt. Rosemary is yet young and dramatic- just two days after she first meets Dick she "cried and cried. 'I love him, Mother··· I never knew I could feel that way about anybody.'" (Fitzgerald, 33) Simultaneously, she is yet naive, and unable as she is to see through the poise of Dick and Nicole Divers whom she admires so much, she is also not experienced enough of an actor to bring the same collected elegance into her own life.

With the progression of the first book, her in-life acting increases significantly. When she begs Dick to sleep with her, she knows that this impulse does not stem from a serious longing to be loved, and she takes it merely as "one of her greatest roles… she flung herself into it more passionately." (Fitzgerald, 96) The extent of the triviality and surrealism of the episode, similar to the detachedness of a play, shows in how she responds to Dick's refusal- "When the door closed she got up and went to the mirror, where she began brushing her hair, sniffling a little." (Fitzgerald, 98-99) Actions of a similarly fictional, created quality continue in how she responds to Dick's later confession of love. "It was time for Rosemary to cry, so she cried a little in her handkerchief." (Fitzgerald, 111) Rosemary's initially "desperate" love for Dick turns out ultimately to be nothing more than a passing scene, an emotional exercise; and she herself is aware of the fact: "Rosemary stood up and leaned down and said her most sincere thing to him: 'Oh, we're such ACTORS- you and I.'" (Fitzgerald, 157)

What has started out as a passing impulse of a dramatic child becomes one of the greatest stages upon which she can display and develop her acting flair. By the end of the book, she has had many such affairs. "She [Rosemary] sang, ' I've slept with six hundred and forty men- if that's the answer you want.' " (Fitzgerald, 312) The distinction between acting and reality has disappeared and the transformation is complete. She welcomes former lover Dick with startling control, "acting amusement, joy, and expectation" (Fitzgerald,

410), and "falling into line" (Fitzgerald, 418) when she croons to Dick about how perfect he is.

If Rosemary is riding on an uphill curve in equalizing reality and acting, then the Divers are surely on a steep downhill plunge. In the beginning, Dick and Nicole Diver are expert manipulators of reality; what seems to Rosemary as an effortlessly perfect life is a painstakingly calculated poise. "Her [Rosemary's] naivete responded whole-heartedly to the expensive simplicity of the Divers, unaware of its complexity and its lack of innocence, unaware that it was··· part of a desperate bargain with the gods and had been attained through struggles she could not have guessed at." (Fitzgerald, 32) Increasingly, however, their ability to keep up pretenses fails. Nicole's mental instability manifests itself, first at a party as a hint that Rosemary is unable to grasp, but later as "a verbal inhumanity that penetrated the keyholes and the cracks in the doors, swept into the suite and in the shape of horror took form again." (Fitzgerald, 166)

Nicole is not the sole problem in their relationship- after Dick's first brief affair with Rosemary, hints of cracks creep across the relationship between Dick and Nicole. "It was a tradition between them that they should never be too tired for anything··· When, inevitably, their spirits flagged they shifted the blame to the weariness and fatigue of others." (Fitzgerald, 142) It is evident that Dick and Nicole do not stay in each other's company for sheer enjoyment but rather for the sake of protecting and maintaining their flawless facade. Yet the fact that the Divers should have to explain their hints of irritation to the reader implies a certain failing in their poise.

In the second book Fitzgerald flashes back to scenes from the past, when Dick and Nicole were young, and his description of their perfect poise then only highlights the completeness of their collapse in the last book. Dick, at age 26, is in his prime, at his "favorite, a heroic period." (Fitzgerald, 170) The crux of his perfection lies in his ignorance of his charm- "he had no idea that he was charming, that the affection he gave and inspired was anything unusual among healthy people." (Fitzgerald, 170)

If what Dick emanates is the appeal of innocence mixed with charisma, what Nicole gives off is necessarily more secretive, given the nature of her past. Starting from the moment she was raped by her father[1], her only response was to "freeze up right away. She'd just say, 'Never mind, never mind, Daddy. It doesn't matter. Never mind.' " (Fitzgerald, 190) Her mental breakdown is what brings her close to Dick in the first place, as doctor and patient, but even in her disturbed state Nicole gathers enough presence of mind to emulate a perfect poise: "she turned coquette and walked away… she felt: There, that'll show him. I've got him, he's mine." (Fitzgerald, 228)

---

1) At first I didn't quite grasp what had happened in the book. A few pages later my brain suddenly sprang back- but I kept on reading numbly. I didn't want to reread it. I didn't return to that part until I read the entire book again. But it was one of those moments that I learned how to deal with embarrassing situations- and not only in books, but in real life as well.

Startling, then, is the sudden breakdown of both Dick and Nicole in the last part of the book. After Dick consummates his relationship with Rosemary, "they [Dick and Nicole] were both restless in the night. In a day or two Dick would try to banish the ghost of Rosemary before it became walled up with them, but for the moment he had no force to do it." (Fitzgerald, 296) Dick, the perfect man, undergoes a series of startling changes: he starts drinking alcohol, and his patience and ability to listen, as well as his manners, also quickly disappear. When he is berated by Mary for having treated her sister-in-law as a servant, he excuses himself saying, "But you've gotten so damned dull, Mary. I listened as long as I could." (Fitzgerald, 384) The once-perfect relationship between Dick and Nicole completely shatters as Nicole finds a new lover in Tommy Barban.

Without this continuous change in the characters, one climbing uphill and the other falling downhill, marking the apparent demise of a character is considerably easier to exaggerate but not as easy to imply. Fitzgerald achieves supremely the distinction of having made Dick Diver a completely tragic hero without sacrificing any of the elegance of the language, which he devotes entirely to condemn the shortcomings of the society in which the Divers and he himself lived. The unique use of juxtaposition increases the impact of the effective message and elevates this book above the simpler works of literature.

Dick Diver

When you read *The Great Gatsby* you fall in love with Gatsby, and when you read *Tender is the Night* you fall in love with Dick Diver. It's inevitable, the way Fitzgerald described those wonderful two men.

For all of Fitzgerald's commendable efforts, however, the fact remains that both of them are utter failures. And Dick is more of a failure than Gatsby is. Gatsby might have used illegal means to gain his wealth, and he might have never achieved the one thing he really wanted, but at least he lost none of his poise. Not even at the very end- he was shot dead by Wilson before that could happen. Whereas with Dick, the reader watches his demise before hearing of his disappearance, and is not even given the solace that Dick has died and that his once-spectacular social grace has gracefully retired. Oscar Wilde wrote, over a hundred years ago: "We live, as I hope you know, Mr. Worthing, in an age of ideals." The statement holds true till today. It is an accurate assessment of the standards of judgment in today's society.

But Dick does not deserve our contempt. He deserves our

gratitude. He is a man who was so intricately tied to his work that he gave up his social persona in order that a patient might be completely cured. We must admit that his patient had a parasitic tendency, and as she clung onto him as his wife she sucked away all the energy that Dick originally had, but the truth remains that Dick was utterly aware of what he was doing- "Dick waited until she was out of sight. Then he leaned his head forward on the parapet. The case was finished. Doctor Diver was at liberty." (Fitzgerald, 438) It was of his own volition, of his own choice.

The fact, then, that society heaps coals on a man who should be one of the paragons of our society, is a sad fact indeed. It does much to testify about the sorrowful state society has come to- a hypocrisy unmatched even in the times of the Pharisees. What we say we admire- a devotion and passion towards one's work- is swept along in disregard when a more important criteria, that of social grace, goes unfulfilled.

When I first read this book I was a sophomore, trembling with the thrill of dreaming about the vivisection of literature. I had friends who shuddered in the same way- sheer delight and ecstatic waiting- when they saw their own areas of passion manifest themselves in some subtle way. Patent rights debates, camera angles in movies, LGBT rights movements. All of us looked forward to the future with the same hard eagerness Dick Diver had, waiting to become people as polished and poised as Diver, to meet with the same type of success that he had initially met with, and to continue it in our own lives.

And when we read of Dick Diver we only saw the flame and fire with which he began his life, but we didn't see the beauty of his passion and his commitment. We did not acknowledge that Diver was perhaps a form of what we might become. We were scared to. We ignored it. And we relegated the entire realm of such commitment to incompetence and stupidity and contemptuously placed him on a level lower than ours.

A message to all of us today, perhaps a message that Fitzgerald didn't quite intend, is that commitment of all type requires sacrifice, and that it should be viewed as valuable and beautiful- and that the reader with true values should be able to recognize his own inadequacies in his responses to the book, and beware of disregarding what might not be incompetence after all.

A Rose for Emily

Introduction

Somewhere from the classroom the sound of a student gagging and retching rang out, and the glib, flat voice that had been reading faltered before it petered out.

"Go on, read it, nice and loud. Don't stop."

At the teacher's command the voice lifted itself again, trembling and wavering, as it hesitantly propelled the last of the words into the waiting air.

"'One of us lifted something from it, and leaning forward, that faint and invisible dust dry and acrid in the nostrils, we saw a long strand of iron-grey hair.'"

From the congregated class a collective moan sounded and indignant mutters scattered the room.

"Oh gross!"

"Isn't that- what do you call it- necrophilia?"

"The very idea- simply- indescribable-"

Mr. Keating grinned at our mutual discomfort.

"Disconcerting, isn't it? So there we have Faulkner, it's a fine exercise in Gothic literature. Have you ever seen anything of this sort?"

The students vigorously shook their heads.

"Is this what you call good literature, Mr. Keating? Really?"

Mr. Keating frowned in mock horror.

"Oh, good heavens, if you don't call this good literature, what is? Remember it's as difficult of a skill to make people repulsed as it is to make them satisfied."

Striding to the blackboard, he took up a piece of chalk and drew three lines, one line slicing the blackboard in half, another curving up, and the last curving down.

"If a story flows along the straight line it's pretty boring through. If it impresses you, gives you a feeling of completion and beauty, it goes up."

He traced the top line again with a piece of red chalk and labeled it GOOD.

"But then there are stories that shock you disgustingly, like this. I don't know, in a way I still think it's kind of beautiful. In a way. Anyhow, when it shocks you, it definitely impacts you. Need examples? Take Thomas Pynchon- a lot of you wouldn't like his books. That is, if you understood them. But it's impossible to deny it still shapes you. It impacts you very strongly. Do you understand?"

He took up the chalk again and traced the bottom line in a bold blue, labeled it IMPRESSIVE, and then he put the chalk to the side and turned to face us again.

"Remember, you don't always have to like the book that touches you. But as long as you're shocked by it, you know it's successful."

A Rose for Emily: Society's Blame

I think most of us have been bullied at one time or another in our lives, and we know how miserable it can get.

Or perhaps not. Maybe you have never been bullied in your life. Maybe you have always had a taut circle of close friends. Congratulations, good for you; now you can try and imagine what it feels like. Ostracization is not fun.

Whichever category you belong to, it doesn't matter. As long as you know what it is.

Join the club.

I used to think that getting bullied was something that applied nearly exclusively to me. After all, when you're the outsider, it seems like everyone else is peering out from the inside. Obviously it's not so, since a lot of my friends have told me similar stories. Dark days, sleepless bright nights, a thirsting ache for laughter and good-humored friendship. The plague that strikes the firstborn of every Egyptian family, but this time it's a few Egyptian families in a city of Jews.

The glances that fall on the victim from the outside are generic. Mostly scornful gazes. Some pitying. And all of them hide a secret gratefulness in the belief that the outsiders and the insiders will never change places.

But everyone responds differently to the same generic gazes. Some victims cling onto the pity of others as if it is the very balm of Gilead. Others would much rather be scorned and spurned than pitied. Some victims silence themselves, enduring, waiting for the painful moments to ease and soothe. Some victims verbalize and diversify in a frenzied attempt to stop from drowning in loneliness. And some victims harden, beginning from their core, growing a thin veneer that repels all touch from the outside world.

I've always been the last type of person- the harsher, prouder type. I will stand outside society but I have to be something nearing a fortress by myself. Waves of sympathy break harder than waves of scorn. The best place to retreat for refuge, unable as I am to reach out to others for help, is necessarily my own self.

With such an identity, then, it is easier to empathize with Emily Grierson, her pride and her obstinacy. Although my sympathy doesn't quite reach the point of agreeing with her necrophiliac tastes, it does allow me to read her story with more leniency, more compassion.

When the world shuts you out from its giant embrace and pounds you with ferocious gazes into a tiny blob of mangled self-respect, the best escape route is to grow a hard coat that mirrors their gazes and gives them back glare for glare. But the prouder you are, the harder it is. There is so much of your identity that you cannot give up but that you have to protect, and the coat grows harder and thicker until it repels even the warmth that tries to seep through the armor.

But being confined to thus limited a space does not give one much scope of control. Whatever seems as if it can be controlled, then, turns into something that must be.

Emily Grierson, in her pathos-filled story, shows us the same. Having been banned all means of self-expression or love by her tyrannical father, Emily lives quietly during the lifetime of the Colonel; after her father's death, however, she searches the opposite type of husband than is expected of a family of her name and status- a Northern railroad overseer. Whenever she speaks, or indeed chooses to make an appearance, her will is always carried out immediately and without dispute. Her cold, steadfast eyes neither waver nor hesitate for any living creature. Unwilling to let her fiance go into the world of death, over which she has no control, she arranges for him to be killed with arsenic, and keeps his body with her until the day of her own death. Such is Emily Grierson- aloof from the world, detached from it, determined to keep herself intact under the thin tight social veneer around her.

Emily's behavior leads me to reflect upon my own. All of us that shy away from social contact in times or hardship, voluntarily or involuntarily, necessarily shy away so as to keep from collapsing. At times like these, then, what is it that we really want? As differently as our social veneers may suggest, don't we secretly long for another person that we can communicate with, a person who will stay by us and watch over us?

I am thankful that I have always had support from my family, and a close group of friends that buoyed me through the harder times. For me another person has always been available for ready and open communication. For me the armor has never had occasion to grow so thick as to entrap me within its folds, and I have never felt an impulse to gain mad domineering control as a way to reaffirm my self-existence and identity. In such a light, Emily's domineering necrophilia is inevitable- it is something that was pushed on her by a society that could not give the proud Southern aristocrat Emily even one friend to help ward off the fear and loneliness of ostracization.

As startling the ending is, and as frightening as it is, the bitterest part of the story lies in the fact that it is invariably the society that has pushed Emily's worst disgrace upon herself, by refusing her even one outlet through which she could have relieved her pent-up and overtaxed emotions.

Their Eyes Were Watching God

Introduction

"Go up to the board and write an author's name. First team to write ten that nobody knows wins. Don't make up any authors, I'm going to check."

The class gave a chorus of good-natured groans.

"Really, Mr. Henderson?"

"Yes, really. Now ready- set- go!"

Three students dashed to the board at once and soon everything was chaos.

"No, no, you idiot, everyone knows Dr. Seuss, settle for something original!"

"Junho, you spelled his name wrong, Pynchon is P-Y-N, not P-I-N!"

"Well, if you know how to spell his name, then I can't write it now can I?"

"Come on, Mirae, make something up!"

"Selena Huh, I heard that!"

By the time three teachers had come to the windows to look their disapproval at the noisy class, the room was at fever pitch.

"There's seven authors up there, and I know five of them. Team A is out, Mr. H!"

"Team A only? All of you are out. These lists are pathetic."

"Who are you kidding, Samuel Langhorne Clemens? You mean Mark Twain! That's cheating, you fraud!"

Pandemonium.

"Everyone STOP!"

Everyone froze and slowly swiveled to the doorway, where the stern Korean voice had come from. The math teacher was standing with a mock frown on his face.

"Never in my life have I heard such a horrendous racket. Henderson, you ought to be ashamed of yourself."

Mr. Henderson stood up, trying to hide his smile.

"Well, we'll try to proceed more quietly, I got carried away. Everyone, back to your seats, and shame on you. Don't you ever read?"

The class waited silently as Mr. Henderson went up to the board and started drawing lines through names.

"I'm just going to cross out the names I'm pretty sure most of you will know. The ones that are left, we'll put to a vote."

We watched as he crossed, crossed, crossed. Suddenly Yuna raised her hand.

"Mr. Henderson, who is Zora Neale Hurston?"

He paused, his hand hovering over the words he had just crossed out, and looked around over his shoulder.

"Zora Neale Hurston? You don't know her?"

"Are we supposed to?"

Mr. Henderson ran a hand through his hair.

"And I was glad because no one put Jane Austen on the board. Hands up everyone who doesn't know Zora Neale Hurston."

More than half the class raised their hands.

"Wow. This really is serious. Tell me something about Hurston, anybody?"

"*Their Eyes Were Watching God.*"

"Who said that just now?"

I slowly raised my head. Everyone was looking at me.

Opening Eyes to a Prejudice:
Their Eyes Were Watching God

It hasn't been very long that I've started reading Black literature. I tried reading one when I was in middle school, *The Color Purple* by Alice Walker. I chose it because I liked the title. That book started me on a two-year abstinence from all Black literature, since I immediately associated the entire category with *Purple*, and thus content of an incomprehensible maturity.

Or at least, I thought so then. When I became a sophomore in high school I read essays by Langston Hughes, poems by Maya Angelou, and books by Toni Morrison. I realized that not all African-American literature was of such an incomprehensible maturity; *Purple* had been just blunter than most of the other books. Of course, there was also the likelihood that I myself had matured, since now I was capable of analyzing most books without blushing, whatever level of maturity they belonged to. Still, the dislike remained. I dutifully read and vivisected everything I was given for homework, but I never enjoyed it.

Indeed, with my childish prejudice, it was little short of a miracle that I managed to begin investigating parts of Black literature that would help me overcome my initial aversion and change it to one of my favorite genres. I was haunting the English library, as I did about twice a day, and Mr. Parry, leaning back in his chair, asked me what I was looking for that afternoon.

"Something I can read while I eat dinner," I replied, "and it can't be *Mansfield Park* since I've read that seven times now."

Mr. Parry shook his head. "You read *Mansfield Park* while you eat dinner? I'll never understand girls. Is there a genre you're looking for?"

"Anything but Black," I replied promptly, and as most of my more enigmatic responses did, the response immediately triggered the question of why. Mr. Parry howled with laughter when he heard my sheepish explanation.

"Yes, *The Color Purple* isn't always suitable for seventh graders," he said, unable to hide a last smirk. "But there are other books, you know, and some of them are very good. I think you'll like this one," and deftly slipping a slim hand into the bookcase he handed me *Their Eyes Were Watching God*.

"I don't really like reading Christian theist books either," I admitted. Mr. Parry laughed again.

"And you honestly think I do? But this one's good, despite its title. It's got nothing to do with Christian theism. It's also Black literature. Read it and tell me what you think of it tonight, because I'm pretty sure you'll finish reading the book before I leave for the night." Mr. Parry winked, and I laughed too. My penchant for skimming books had grown to become something of a legend and Mr. Parry often teased me about it.

As Mr. Parry had foretold, I did finish the book before he left- I finished it before the dinner hour was over, though my dinner itself was left more than half uneaten. The book was like nothing I had expected: it was sweet and beautiful in an old-fashioned way, and throbbing with true love, not the temporary love that the suffering sometimes use to escape from their tortures, but a love that was real and true and touched the drawstrings of the heart.

Hurston's book deals with a love that all of us are able to understand, not an estrangement that only the estranged are able to empathize with, and that is why her book, to me, was so much more powerful than all of the other pieces of Black literature that I had read.

Let us first consider *Beloved* or *Bluest Eye*, by Toni Morrison. Both deal with the excruciating emotional pain that the protagonists are put through because of their race- the aftereffects of slavery that has a worse effect on the mind than on the beleaguered body.

In such books the authors show that according to what Blacks have been treated as, they have thus become. Slaves are treated by their masters as if they are animals; consequently, bestiality rules them, body and soul. Lovemaking becomes no more than the mating of animals that, having succumbed to their libido, eagerly participate in sexual intercourse only for the cathartic pleasure lovemaking provides. It becomes an escape route, a way to push away and forget the physical and spiritual pains of slavery and prejudice. Since it is used for something else- a release- than for true love, lovemaking becomes degraded.

In Hurston's work, however, love is treated preciously and kindly. The protagonist Janie Crawford passes through three husbands, not from a bestial longing for a way to relieve pent-up stress and desire, but from a forlorn, humane longing to meet someone who truly loves her for who she is. In her third husband, Tea Cake, she finally finds a man who loves her not only as a trophy wife but as a human being whose thoughts can be expressed, and it is with Tea Cake and Janie that the reader's sympathy remains until after the closure of the book.

It is important to note here that Hurston neither silences nor ignores the racial prejudice Blacks face. All along there is an implication that the Blacks' social plane of life is forced to a level completely below that of the whites', although the story focuses entirely on the former plane without giving the latter plane much chance for interaction. Foils that appear in the book show marked prejudice against the African-American community and for the white one, and are duly reviled by the readers. Hurston does not idealize the idea of love within her race by closing her eyes to the reality.

What the author of *Their Eyes* does instead is to show that the people of the Black community are as spiritually completed and healthy as those of the white community, and thus deserve the same type of respect as the white gets. Hurston, as a sedate Black woman writing of and in a somewhat stabilized Black community, has written a novel that, to borrow her own words, avoids being "a treatise on sociology"- a scathing epithet that would pithily characterize nearly every other piece of Black literature at the time. But this is why Hurston has been largely ignored for the last three decades: her peaceful realism, an unprecedented writing style for a Black writer, drew her into the realms of oblivion. As Walker says in her biography of Hurston, Hurston is the champion of the excellent racial health of Black community- "a sense of black people as complete, complex, undiminished human beings, a sense that is lacking in so much black writing and literature."

Later that night Mr. Parry asked me how far I had gotten on in the book, and when I told him that the book was over and finished with, he clapped in mock delight and, admittedly, with a faint trickle of real pride.

"How did you like it?" he asked as we headed to our classes.

"I loved it!" I exclaimed. "It's such a beautiful story! I'm so sorry Tea Cake had to die, though. I love him. Such a charming character!"

Mr. Parry nodded his satisfaction. "I thought you'd like him. Did you try comparing the book with other pieces of Black literature yet?"

I shook my head slowly. "Not really. Does it go into Black literature only because a Black person wrote it, or are there any similarities between the works of other Black writers and this novel that makes this Black literature?"

The teacher turned his head to watch my reaction as we continued strolling down the hallway. "What do you think?"

"I feel like most other pieces of Black literature were too depressing for this to go into the same category."

Mr. Parry tsk-tsked disapprovingly. "Looks like I'll have a lot to teach you. Have you read Langston Hughes's essay yet, "Salvation"? That's also Black literature, but there's not even a hint of the depressing there. Asian literature can't only talk about- oh, the Three Kingdoms, or Amy Tan's chop suey. It encompasses anything that talks about Asian culture."

We had arrived at my classroom now, and Mr. Parry had another two flights of stairs to climb down and another stretch of hallway to walk, but he stayed his steps and continued talking as he pushed the sliding door open for me like a gentleman. "It's very important to remember, the only way Black writers can't write Black literature is if they talk about a segment of life that is entirely disparate from their own. Which, in writing, is impossible, since even fantasies are based off the realities of the present.

"It's true that sometimes Black literature is credited with a lot more of the miserable sexual vignettes, but that's because their entire history has been spent in subjugation, and one of the few ways it can be expressed is through something that needs no education to know. Hurston wrote about a part of Black life that not many people think of, because it's a part that seems too happy to have to write about. When you've got the bad parts in your life along with the good and you have to write, or you want to write, you'll find that you'll nearly always go for the bad- first of all, you feel it more acutely, and it's so hard to be thankful for the good at times like those; and second of all, the bad has more pathos. The reader understands more. Now is that a good habit, necessarily? No. But is it a powerful writing style? Hell yes.

"I can see why you'd like reading Hurston so much. Granted, compared to *The Color Purple*, or even *Song of Solomon*, it's much more convenient to read- much more universal, much lighter. But the harsher the reading is, the more gravity it has. Understand? No? Well, you've still got time."

I watched Mr. Parry walk off into the darkened hallway, heard his steps fade off into the staircase, and taking a deep breath, I stepped over the doorway.

Beloved

Dearly Beloved:
The Supernatural Aspects of Toni Morrison's Works

There is something vaguely sinister about Toni Morrison's works, that doesn't quite reach the reader at first, but as time passes, it slowly becomes more and more palpable.

In a way it reminds me of a movie I watched once.

I don't remember the plot any more, just a vague looming figure hidden by the mist. It must have been a horror movie. At first the light and the mist combine to make a thick swirling haze that conceals and disguises the figure. And it seems nothing more than a friendly mass in the distance. But then the light slowly grows brighter and the mist recedes, the last tendrils of the haze uncurling and melting into clarity, and suddenly, the figure is exposed, massive and threatening. It arrests you, in your spot, fixes you, and renders you motionless. Frightening, definitely; and powerful and hypnotizing.

Mirae once told me that Morrison's writing style was "distinctly alluring, distinctly captivating, and distinctively disturbing." I hadn't read any of her works yet, then, so I didn't know, but Mirae's verdict stayed with me when I first picked up *Beloved* to try and read it. I didn't realize what she had meant until I saw in my mind's eye a quiet soft girl in a dress of white gliding into a room, and then instinctively, a fragment of a recurring nightmare in my head- a dark massive figure, giant and looming under the light. Then I understood what she had meant.

Toni Morrison's style is definitely distinct. Compared to Alice Walker, or even Zora Neale Hurston, she narrates in a much more sensitive, descriptive, and clean-cut way. The thoughts and the fleeting emotions of individuals have been captured and immortalized in perceptive and significant phrases.

The fact that Morrison chooses to use a wholly elegant form of syntax and diction is significant: while her style somewhat distances us from the continuous thrumming of reality and pain that the Black dialogue is so apt at communicating, it produces an enhanced effect of the equality between Blacks and whites. By mutedly fleshing out the poignancy of the pain that the Blacks underwent, through a wholly removed third-person narrative rather than the emotionally invested first-person narrative form, Morrison manages to objectively delineate the crushing humbling that the Blacks' pride had to undergo. She gently reminds the reader that the inhumane treatment the whites forced on the Blacks was undeserved, and she draws attention to the noble slaves who patiently and quietly waited for liberation.

By the "wholly removed third-person narrative" I do not mean that Morrison's characters are detached from their reality, or that the narrative is unsympathetic to their thoughts. I mean that the narrator is able to see the scene and the emotional quality of the characters' feelings with more clarity and sensitivity than the characters themselves. In a way she is like the Edith Wharton, or the Scott Fitzgerald, of the Blacks: the elusive qualities of the era, and the vague swirl of emotions, have all been preserved in her excellent choice of words. For the most part of the narration her words are like those of a poet speaking in terms of memory about events past, with a certain blurry quality that reaches the readers in the same way that their own memories come to them after years of neglect and forgetfulness. When a poet who has already proven her skill with words adds slight additional aberrations to her grammar, the aberrations merely act as further testimony to her skill.

Among the many themes she communicates in her complex works, a prominently figuring one is that of subtle terror, probably something often felt among the Blacks who were forced into slavery. In each of her different books Morrison accomplishes it in a different way, but in *Beloved* the factor of terror figures more largely than others, and it shows from the title. The figure causing that vague terror is the titular character.

What about *Beloved* is so frightening? From the very beginning the book starts, "124 was spiteful. Full of a baby's venom." (Morrison, 3) And all throughout the first chapters the book continuously mentions the ghost of a baby, raging and hot-tempered, and it throws the audience into a kind of turmoil. *Beloved* is not a horror story, and Morrison introduces the ghost in too matter-of-fact a manner for it to have the right suspense and terror; but we also know that the events happening in the book would not be possible unless- unless ghosts really existed. Unless the ghost of a baby really was haunting Sethe's house. The reader shivers.

But then there are many things that happen in the lives of the Blacks that are terrifying and incomprehensible. When Sethe was planning to run away, she had a newborn baby, and because she didn't want it to suffer from slavery she killed the baby herself. Sethe is a strong, hard woman, with "iron-hard eyes", but the death of her baby has crippled her with a guilt that clings onto her stubbornly. It has even more tenacity than the last symbol of her slavery- the chokecherry tree that sprouted on her back after her last whipping. In the first few chapters Morrison subtly brings out her remorse, highlighting bloodstained colors to emphasize the drabness and thus the desperation of her guilt: "Every dawn she saw the dawn, but never acknowledged or remarked its color. There was something wrong with that. It was as though one day she saw red baby blood, another day the pink gravestone chips, and that was the last of it." (Morrison, 39)

But later, after her old friend and new lover Paul D has frightened the baby out of the house with his careening rage, a new face appears on the scene- a girl with a white dress, who names herself Beloved. At first there are only suspicions; later the suspicions are confirmed: Beloved is the baby's ghost in real life, and since it is real, it is a ghost that Paul D can no longer frighten out. The fears that are contained within the mind are controllable, but after they grow real they become uncontrollable. The victims must live conquered by their own fears.

Slowly Beloved overpowers Sethe. Her consuming love is sapping the life out of Sethe, who, apologetic and remorseful, cannot help but try and give more and more to the baby whom she once tried to kill. The last action of a selfless love has come back to haunt and chase into the grave. The Hammurabian code of eye for eye, life for life comes out here. Since Beloved has come back to life, either Beloved must return to her death, or Sethe must die in her place instead.

The book ends with Beloved melting back into the shadows-"Remembering seemed unwise⋯ So they forgot her. Like an unpleasant dream during a troubling sleep." (Morrison, 522). Sethe is a broken woman, unable to comprehend her worth or regain her fiery purpose to live. Paul D says, "You your best thing, Sethe," but Sethe can only dumbly reply, "Me? Me?" The memory of the ghost has completely broken her.

But Beloved is more than merely the memory of a ghost. It is a crippling legacy of slavery, the horrifying extents that slavery can drive a mother to, and the aftereffects of the events that never leave a slave- not physically, but mentally. And this legacy is still necessarily named Beloved, because it is something that has been so tied into the life of the slaves that it is inextricable and has become their life. Once a slave, always a slave. Once crippled, always crippled.

Distinctly alluring, distinctly captivating, and distinctively disturbing, is what Mirae said. I believe it. Mirae was right. Toni Morrison's soulful narrative of a story with no happy ending is exactly how things happen in reality, and thus is all the more unnerving and devastating. In short, the story is disturbing because it is true. That such tragedies should have had to happen is a sad reflection on the humanity that forced them to come about.

Through the Looking- Glass

Introduction

When I was in eighth grade I joined the Drama club and our first assignment was to adapt a scene from a play or a movie. I was in the same group with Sewook then, and since both of us were famous for being the least movie-knowledgeable two people in the entire school the rest of the group ignored us for the most part and planned out what they were going to do.

Just then there was a universal Alice rage, since the new Tim Burton movie had just come out, and it was this movie that the group decided to adapt. I was to act Alice, and Sewook was to act the Hatter. I honestly wanted to base it off the book but the group insisted that I watch the movie and learn my part from the movie instead.

I remember the first time I watched it I clung onto Yeonjae's arm with a force she didn't approve of. "Your nails aren't long," she said matter-of-factly, "but they hurt. What's so scary about it, anyways? That's just what Wonderland is supposed to be like."

I looked at her with new interest sparkling in my eyes- or at least, that's how Sewook described it, since he wasn't really watching the movie, either; he was having more fun watching me get freaked out by the settings.

"Wonderland is supposed to be like- this?"

Yeonjae snorted. "Yes, you innocent. It's forests and rooms underground. Did you expect the sunlight to come shining through?"

It wasn't because it was a Burton movie; it was because it was Wonderland. I turned to Sewook, who was snickering as loudly as it was possible to snicker with seven other irate movie-lovers in the room. "Don't laugh, you. Wonderland?"

Sewook shrugged. "Let's have fun making a crazy Hatter and a weird Alice. What do you say?"

Through the Looking- Glass
of Lewis Carroll's Works

There is something tantalizing about Lewis Carroll's works that invariably entices the reader to come back to read them a second time, and then a third- an incredibly sharp and pungent wit that satisfies the elementary level with its obvious nonsense, but intrigues the more mature stages with its mysterious depth. But then Carroll's work ages with the reader. It's like Tim Burton's movies: seen by elementary students they are bright and flashy and fascinating pieces of art, but the older the viewers grow, the more able they become, to notice the fascinatingly ominous implications of the settings.

Whenever I read *Through the Looking-Glass* I am reminded of the time I first saw Burton's "*Charlie's Chocolate Factory.*" I was in eighth grade then, and we had just finished our midterms, so our English teacher lent the movie to our class for a day so that we could watch it through. For most of the kids it was a childish movie that they barely remembered watching but remembered enjoying, so they clapped and laughed as they watched it. I was sitting between Yeonjae and Sewook, who both happened to be prototypes of the silent movie-watching type. But the unnerved glances I kept throwing them moved them sufficiently out of their concentration to talk.

Sewook was the first one to notice. "What is it?"

"Why is everyone laughing?" I hissed.

Yeonjae snorted. "Because it's childish. Look!" The Oompa-Loompas had just finished singing and dancing about Augustus Gloop. "What do you think that is?"

I stared at her blankly for a while. "You think this movie is childish."

Yeonjae looked at me with a duh-are-you-crazy look, while

Sewook looked at me with a more patient I-think-I-might-get-you look. I struggled for the words.

"Doesn't something kind of creep you out here? The- the colors, Johnny Depp's laugh- it's just all so weird. I don't get why this is a children's movie. It's not. It should be for teenagers, in the very least."

I should note that incidentally, it was the first time I had seen any of Burton's works, and the implicit darkness scared me more than any outright horror could, like a cold that doesn't buffet you with wind but instead seeps into the marrow of your bones and leaves you drained and shivering and colder.

Sewook nodded. "Yeah, there was a kind of weird feeling, but I was trying to shake it off. When I was little I thought this was the greatest movie, you know? So it wouldn't make sense that this was getting kind of creepy…"

Yeonjae opened her mouth to speak, closed it, opened it again, and then settled back in her chair to watch the movie. I thought she was going to get cranky if we kept talking during the movie, so Sewook and I talked in whispers in the beginning. But soon the three of us were constantly pointing out incongruences in the movie- "What type of color scheme is that for innocent children?" "These punishments are really gruesome, if you ask me. Like some fanciful torture…" "These Oompa-Loompas are- sordid! Don't laugh," Sewook said defensively as Yeonjae and I looked at each other and then cracked up. "I can't think up of a better word to explain them."

But the word was right, somehow, the same way it is right to describe some of the scenes in Lewis Carroll's works. The reason the two are similar is because they both use the same concept: they peek into the world of adults through childish means. *Charlie's Chocolate Factory*, for example, deals with the aftereffects of repression through the crazy chocolate genius Willie Wonka; *Alice in Wonderland* deals with identity and surrealism in a similar manner. This has the effect that a child, unconscious of the realities of what is being reflected, merely thinks both to be enchanting, funny pieces; but an adult is able to notice the more subtle messages that the author is trying to communicate in either work.

Carroll's Modernism and Surrealism were anachronistic themes for the era in which they were written, but there was a sensibility in his experiments that brought his works recognition not only as children's stories but as adult masterpieces as well. Whether Carroll truly intended his works to be for children or for adults is uncertain. If it was meant in the least for adults, however, then it is obvious that the slightly dreamy worldview that acts as the fundamental basis for both of his plots carries a clear, intentional message and is no device that simply allows the fanciful Alice stories to take place. Perhaps, through his works, Carroll was trying to communicate a view that would not have been kindly taken at his time.

A question that continues throughout the entire book- in fact, the very question the plot seeks to answer throughout- is the identity of Alice. *Alice* is often viewed as a Modernist work due to the surrealism of the book, the fantastic occurrences that take up the bulk of the episodes; and if the book is surrealistic then Alice can only be taken as the bridge that ties the surreal world to the real world.

But what if the book is instead based off another idea? Let us inspect solipsism, an idea expounded by the seventeenth-century French philosopher Renee Descartes. His philosophy states that the only thing one can be sure of existing is one's mind; hence his famous quote, "I think, therefore I live." All of Alice's travels in the Looking-Glass World, as well as in Wonderland, could as well be described by solipsism as by surrealism, since everything is entirely contained within the occurrences of her imagination. Carroll's worldview is reflected in the Unicorn's quote, when he first sees Alice and thinks her to be a fabulous monster: "Well, now that we have seen each other, if you'll believe in me, I'll believe in you." (Carroll, 237) The mind, again, is all that matters. Although Descartes intended his philosophy to establish the mind as a single starting point so that we could base off it our observations of the world around us, and Carroll definitely seems to have taken solipsism to the other extreme, it still functions as a plausible conjecture to what the worldview behind this book might have been. Then Carroll's philosophy could be neatly summarized into the social critic and stand-up comedian Bill Hick's quote: "Today a young man on acid realized that all matter is merely energy condensed to a slow vibration, that we are all one consciousness experiencing itself subjectively, there is no such thing as death, life is only a dream, and we are the imagination of ourselves."

Around the end of *Through the Looking-Glass*, however, another part of Carroll's philosophy manifests itself in Alice's conversation with Tweedledum and Tweedledee about the sleeping Red King, which throws doubt onto the former idea Carroll seems to have suggested throughout the plot. Tweedledum and Tweedledee maintain that Alice is only a part of the Red King's dream and therefore unreal. "I am real!" Alice defends herself, laughing through her tears at the ridiculousness of the situation and saying that she wouldn't be able to cry were she unreal, to which Tweedledum replies contemptuously that her tears can't possibly be real.

It is not a play on words, but instead a play on philosophy: what happens to Alice if she is the dream of her imagination? Does every figment of the imagination indeed exist somewhere, provide a manifestation in some remote universe that our minds control? Or are we simply the imagination of some other figure, of which we sometimes dare imagine?

But queerly enough this is actually one of the more sensible parts of the novel's philosophy. Everything seems so fantastic that it makes better sense for Alice to be a part of a fictional character's dream, a character who we know to have no real identity- the Red King. It is easier than believing that Alice might be a real child. And it is easier to believe that the story is not a part of a real living human child's imagination, but the living reality of a fictional character such as the Red King. Looking again at *Alice in Wonderland* and *Through the Looking-Glass*, it is somewhat inconceivable that a real child, a real little girl, would be able to dream such dreams. Alice would have to be a drug addict suffering from hallucinations.

The devices of children's nursery rhymes and the chessboard game also play a large effect in throwing Carroll's message into clearer focus. All the characters that Alice meets, such as Tweedledum and Tweedledee, the Lion and the Unicorn, and Humpty Dumpty, act accordingly to the rhymes. Every time they do so, they make it clear that they are doing it on account of the rhyme, even if they do not directly mention it. They are acting under the orders of a power above them.

The chess game, too, is a classic example of God's control over mankind. His is the Hand that moves the pieces, and ours the pawns that obey His movements. In such a chessboard there are two queens, two kings, and the given numbers of bishops and knights and pawns as given in the book, and they move according to the rules of chess.

But there is a sense of rebellion in this book that seems ever-present, however faint it is. The characters of the rhymes know how the rhymes turn out for the most part, and they're aware that everything is part of an endless routine. Alice herself is a part of a walking inconsistency, since there are only supposed to be two queens in a game of chess, but by passing through all the squares she becomes a third queen. Ultimately it is due to this third queen that the Looking-Glass World comes tumbling down back into Alice's original world.

The story, then, seems like a battle on Carroll's part, against the religious worldviews that we are under the control of a great Divine Power above us. By making his characters acting under the rhymes but simultaneously aware that they are the pawns of the rhymes, and by making a third queen appear and bring a world that is her imagination come tumbling down, Carroll denies the fact that any other power is greater than ours. His imagination made Alice's Wonderland and Looking-Glass-land real. It is ultimately our imagination that makes the world real.

Before I had a teacher who continuously warned us of the dangers of over-interpretation in literature. "There are times when the author says, for example, that a room is blue," he said once. "The English teacher takes it to mean depression, thoughtfulness, contemplation, morbidity. Because that's what blue means, in the color interpretation scheme. Whereas the author seriously thinks, hello, the room was just damn blue."

I fear that in interpreting Carroll's works I have experimented too much without knowing what the author's true intentions were. But if these are the impressions that I received, then I trust that I won't be the only one.

Atlas Shrugged & The Fountainhead

Introduction

Last time I was skimming the Jokes section of the school newspaper, and since it had been Valentine's Day just the Friday of the week before, there was a whole series of puns related to love. I passed over most with a faint smile, but there was one that stalled me from discarding the paper: "Be your own valentine- Love, Ayn Rand." I fairly howled. My friends wanted to know what I was laughing so hard over, but as I learned the hard way, it's difficult to appreciate that pun unless you've had something against Ayn Rand for as long as I have.

Ayn Rand and I go back a long way. When I was a freshman I had to read *The Fountainhead* for homework. Incensed by the philosophy revealed in the book, I complained to another teacher, who empathized with me but recommended me to gain more grounds on which I could base off and validate my arguments. Thus it came that I picked up *Atlas Shrugged*, a book that not many people would choose to read in their free time.

But it helped, since when I became a sophomore it was mandatory to take a philosophy course that met for class once a week. It was largely student-led and the only assignment was for students to come up with and prepare for a presentation that they would give in front of the class at the end of the semester, speaking about a train of philosophy they were interested in. I wanted to do an analysis of a philosophy that I was already familiar with, so I suggested researching Objectivism. As we had trickled into groups for the project, there was a supposedly even and untiring division of labor, but the only two who contributed were Selena and I. We were also the only two who *could* contribute- the rest of the group members had largely given up in the middle of the book last year.

But Selena and I forgot about it as time passed. Gradually the hour allotted for presentation preparation slowly turned into the test-prep hour as midterms, then APs, began looming. With school tests and standardized tests swamping our schedules, the philosophy presentation was pushed to the very back of our minds. It was only after we finished all our APs that Selena and I found the time to frantically throw together a paper and a Prezi presentation on objectivism and why it wouldn't work.

Although I really hated reading the book when I had to read it, today I'm all too thankful that I had to read it. Objectivism remains a scintillating example of what not to believe in, and how not to behave. All of us go through an enlarging experience sometime in our lives. Sometimes we really hate the lesson, but after it's over we admit grudgingly that it was one of the most precious lessons that could be learned. Mine was Objectivism.

Why Objectivism Doesn't Work

"Are you going to summarize *Atlas Shrugged*?"

Selena was crouched over her iPad, her black Prada glasses perched on the tip of her nose where they had slid down to after a couple hours of continuous typing. She glanced at me briefly, but her glance was more like a glare.

"I didn't even read it, and you want me to summarize it?"

"You have Sparknotes!"

"Sparknotes? Sparknotes! You read the book, for heaven's sake!"

We looked at each other and burst out laughing. Selena threw her iPad down on her lap and stretched back. I rubbed my temple with my fingers as I thought.

"Okay, Lena, let's do it like this. You introduce Ayn Rand, define objectivism, and attack the economic impact. I'll explain the impact of objectivism on the microcosmic scale and the macrocosmic scale. I think it'll be okay if I explain the microcosmic scale with *The Fountainhead* and the macrocosmic one with *Atlas Shrugged*."

"Which means you will be summarizing both. Yes?"

"I hate you. Yes."

"Perfect. Hang on. That means I do the Prezi?"

"Do you really trust me with anything related to computers?"

Selena hid a smile as she shook her head emphatically. "Nope. Sorry for mentioning it. I'm doing the Prezi."

I laughed quietly to myself as I continued typing. Selena was quiet for a while, but she suddenly burst out with a shout.

"Ha! Hey, look at this. There's a Colbert Report on Ayn Rand. Must be because of that entire Mitt Romney and Paul Ryan fiasco. This is going to be fun."

Having no idea who- or what- Colbert was, I kept typing silently. Selena snickered to herself as she watched the video clip, saved it and captioned it, then went on to work on the Prezi presentation. About an hour passed in silence.

"Hey, I think I'm done. Want to read over what I've got?"

Selena leaned back lazily from where she was working.

"Why don't you explain what you've got? I think it'll be faster, and honestly, I don't want to read another typed word."

I shrugged. "It's going to be long, but you asked for it."

Selena smirked and put down her iPad. I cleared my throat and started reading.

"So objectivism is a philosophy where the human reason reigns supreme. Everything relies on the individual's ability to think clearly and logically about what will directly benefit himself. The investment of emotions, then, becomes an unwanted hampering factor. This necessarily means that the individual will only agree to actions that directly benefits himself. Altruism and sacrifice all become a waste of resource and time. Sentiment is cheap."

"The next determining factor is necessarily judging exactly how applicable this philosophy is. For the individual, it must be said that objectivism is not an unworthy goal to pursue. Especially considering the trends that today's society flows in. Today many people sacrifice parts of their identity in order to conform better to the world in general. We often hear the term "cookie-cutter" today. This is because so many people are generic, cut by the same cookie mold. They force themselves to become generic in order to be liked and accepted. In such circumstances individuality is not only welcome, it is crucially necessary.

"And simultaneously, the twin problems of identicalness and genericness bring about a third problem of irresponsibility. Anyone that is unwilling to stand out will necessarily be afraid to take any responsibility onto his shoulders, in the fear that whatever he is being held responsible for might not succeed. Productivity lags. Success disappears. Society collapses.

"Rand produces a supposedly superhero response to these faults, teaching us that what the other people think is not important. Only what I think about myself is important. And whatever I do, as long as it gives me pleasure or it benefits me, will be the right thing to do. The character Howard Roark, protagonist of *The Fountainhead*, shows this idea the best. The society closes in on him, trying to break him into submission, but Roark refuses to adhere to what is socially accepted. The antagonist of the story is, of course, an altruist whose benevolent facade securely covers a mad desire to obliterate all individuality in the world.

"As a character by himself, Roark is rather admirable. He sticks to what he thinks is good, and he does not let other people decide what is good for him. Since he is not afraid he is also willing to take responsibility for whatever he thinks to be right and good. The microcosmic aspect of objectivism is quite positive.

"But it is obvious that Roark is only admirable in his exclusivity. Simply put, if there was a society comprised entirely of people like Roark, firstly, Roark would cease to be admirable, and secondly, such a society would not be a good one, or a smoothly functioning one. In fact, it would not be a society at all.

"Objectivism, on the macrocosmic level, contains two fundamental discrepancies that make it impossible as a candidate for a universal philosophy. First of all is that the objectivist philosophy, in its very definition, opposes the fundamental constituents of society. Secondly is the fact that the objectivist philosophy is necessarily limited to a select few. It is always a comparatively elite philosophy and thus can never apply to the comparatively lower classes on the intellectual scale.

"Firstly, inspecting the fundamental discrepancy between the definitions of objectivism and society. Objectivism firstly implies that whatever society pursues is of secondhand worth, and what the individual pursues is of the best quality. The individual must always reject the values of society in order to aggrandize his achievements. If objectivism has such a prejudiced view of the inferiority of society in comparison to the individual, it would be foolish to imagine a society that conforms well to objectivist values.

"In tandem with the flow of the thought, since whatever the individual pursues is necessarily better than what the society strives for, objectivism implies that the society must always be sacrificed for the individual- or that the individual and society stand on opposite poles. In short, the objectivist needs society as a backdrop against which he may be contrasted as to stand in clearer focus, but the two can never coexist.

"Not only that, but objectivism also scorns altruism as being of utter worthlessness, as it gives the individual no direct benefit. Every well-run society leans heavily on altruism- it is the motor that allows societies to function. There is a maxim that says "it is love that makes the world go around." Like all maxims, it contains at least a grain of truth. In a world filled with people unwilling to help one another, unless direct benefits are included, what type of society can exist? Can the random grouping of people that will appear possibly be called a society?

"Secondly, considering the scope of people to which the idea of objectivism may be open. An interesting fact about Ayn Rand's books is that all of them are severely idealistic: not a single character who might be remotely stupid ever enters the book. All the men are proud, tall, austere, clever- no, not merely clever; they are geniuses. The women are all slender and beautiful and altogether desirable, and all the women use their bodies shamelessly in a pursuit of finding their true identity. No one ugly or stupid can ever be an objectivist.

"The most excellent example of the representation of objectivism in the macrocosmic sense is in Rand's *Atlas Shrugged*, an antithetic book in that it undermined the very cause it was striving to uphold. In *Atlas*, the main character is Dagny Taggart, the queen of the country's largest railroad company. She has no time for emotions and pity but plenty of time for love affairs- with Francisco d'Anconia, the prince of copper; Hank Rearden, the king of steel; and John Galt, emperor of motors. The people that she meets with and loves are all supremely talented and those with only mediocre ability can never hope to be included in her sphere of recognition.

"There are several major faulty premises in *Atlas*, that relates not only to the supreme surrealism of the plot, but also to the impossibility of objectivism to be applied to the real world. For one, the book takes for granted that there is no human that lies between the two extremes of talent and lack of it. But the real world is not so perfectly cut. Sometimes there are characters of middling talent and middling individuality. They will be overshadowed by those with phenomenal talent, and they will be cowed by those with scintillating individuality. Perhaps those that have lost all will for individuality to the point that they wish to have to take on no responsibilities, have lost the fundamental importance that makes them human. But what about those failures who have failed simply due to lack of ability? Do they deserve to be swept into that same category of incompetence and irresponsibility? Surely not.

"The second discrepancy lies in something more intricately tied to the plot itself. In the story Dagny Taggart flits from one lover to another, falling head over heels in love with every new sight of perfection that she can see. Disregarding the curiosity that every such perfect man in the world could deem her the most beautiful and most desirable woman, the detachedness with which the men give up Dagny is marvelous and thus unrealistic. Either what they first felt for Dagny was not love, or their actions after having lost Dagny are masks of what they truly feel, which seems to be what all perfect people despise. It is definitely an incongruence that lies heavily within the respective fictional characters of Hank Rearden and Francisco d'Anconia, but it seems to serve as proof for the extent of how unrealistic objectivism is.

"Thirdly, *Atlas Shrugged* is a what-if spun on the talented and the perfect going on strike. The title captures the story perfectly: the talented elites, who support the world with their arms of talent and money, feel the burden of the free-riders too heavy. They shrug. They refuse to work at the terms of the world until the world begins to work at their terms. The book ends when the existing society of looters who aggrandized their riches through no work of their own collapses. Their point has been made, after all; without the determined and the talented to back up the re-allocators of wealth society will necessarily meet its economic demise.

"And what happens when these people actually do go back? Is there any guarantee that these people will make a better society than what is pre-existent? How are we to believe it? Are these the type of people who would willingly give up their money so that the financially unable can reach a point of financial ability? No, these are the type of people that would turn up their heads in such circumstances. That's your problem, they would say, I began lower down than you. Find your own way out. Get the lowest of jobs, and work your way up. I trained that way too. They never think that they were never in a state when they could not possibly think of working. They do not think of the people who are too tired to move another step. They find no way to help the socially desperate and the socially indifferent. Those people, their proud stance suggests, would be better off dying.

"What then? What type of unforgiving society would we have accomplished in making? A society that disapproves of sympathy and altruism as being of the basest of emotions? Is that a society worth having? And thus we return to the resolution that the fundamental definition of society is incompatible with objectivism-with the conviction that we are right.

"Like most ideas, objectivism is a double-edged sword. Unlike most ideas, however, one of the sides is too deadly for comfort. Although it may sometimes be helpful for the individual, it is absolutely lethal for the society. Objectivism is a philosophy that will not succeed well in reality.

The Adventures of Huckleberry Finn

Why Huck Is Not Racist

As renowned of a literary masterpiece as *The Adventures of Huckleberry Finn* is, it has received far more than its fair share of criticism. Various pieces of constructive- or not so constructive-criticism comes flying from all across its wide spectrum of readers: the plot is shoddily constructed; the characters are forced; the style is crude and narrowly escapes vulgarity.

And, truth be told, some of these criticisms actually are plausible. The ending is rather disappointing, and when Tom reappears as the impractical romantic, he has been so forced into a narrow box of a stereotype that he has lost all naturalness- there is no Tom anymore; just a faceless romanticist holding the name Tom. The syntax is rich and flowing with the warm good-natured drawl of a young Southerner boy, and personally it is one of the most enchanting parts of Twain's prose, but if you don't like it then you don't. That is a matter of taste.

But there is one key criticism that still hasn't lost its voice over the years despite its sheer absurdity. It is the issue of racism. Every year we see so many authors combat over the discriminatory aspects of *Huck Finn*. Please, let us be mature, and open our eyes to facts, truths, and logic: *Huck Finn* is in no way a racist book, and its characters and its diction prove it.

It is true that Huck does not quite treat Jim with the same respect with which he would treat adults, or even people of his own age. He enjoys explaining things to Jim, as an adult might to a little child, and sometimes he plays pranks on Jim as well. Critics immediately wave red flags at such parts, noting that the hierarchy that Huck takes for granted is an implicit promotion of racism. Since a reader generally comes to view through the protagonist's eyes the world that a book communicates, the fact that our protagonist Huck Finn condones slavery and racism, is tantamount to a claim on Mark Twain's part that both are justified.

I remember a certain striking example, a piece of criticism by a college student, who claimed in her article that Huck Finn's racist perspective and disgust of Blacks was manifested in his words, "I never saw such a nigger." She remarked that the racist comment was more than ample proof for Huck's irritation at Jim's inherent 'stupidity' as a Black. I was in the middle of writing a timed essay during class at the time, but I couldn't help laughing out loud at the inconsistency evident in the woman's argument.

Let us imagine our grandfathers. One is loving and kind; he likes telling his grandchildren stories and smoking pipes. Now Grandpa is being stubborn about something. Perhaps he does not like dark meat on the Thanksgiving turkey; perhaps he wants to watch the Macy's parade instead of the Super Bowl. If we roll our eyes and exclaim, "I never saw such an adult!" can we be said to be making a discriminatory remark? We are definitely condemning him, but are we condemning him because he is an adult? The obvious answer is no. On the contrary, we are saying that he should be acting more like an adult, since his behavior would be an aberration from the generally faultless exterior that most grownups show. In the same way Huck is not making a racist remark, except for perhaps the use of the word- which will be discussed later on- but he is excusing Jim's ignorance as being uncharacteristic of other Blacks. He is promoting the general good sense that Blacks show.

I believe most of the contentions that the critics have to make could be rebutted in such a way, but since it will take too long, I will condense my rebuttal into two major arguments: that firstly, a certain era's social mores cannot help but largely influence a book written in the time period unless it is a utopian or dystopian work; and secondly, that Huck is still a child and the book draws his development and not his fully-developed philosophy.

My first argument, that an era's social mores will naturally largely influence a book of the time. This is a rather obvious piece of logic. Literature is ultimately a representation of society that has exaggerated a certain part in order to communicate a certain message. Mark Twain, in order to establish a credible, realistic, empathetic world, could not help but include in his work the racist shortcomings of the South. I doubt that Twain would have been able to make a living otherwise- it is not easy to like a work that disagrees with us in too fundamental a part of our social structure.

But the probing reader is led to conclude: it is obvious that Twain seeks to deal with the issue of slavery in some way, since the main plot revolves around a slave's escapade from his mistress. What, then, is he seeking to communicate? It might be that by highlighting the thoughtless inhumanity of slavery, and by mocking the inconsistencies behind it, Twain is trying to criticize it.

Examples of this are rampant. When Huck first searches for help, he finds a Mrs. Loftus who believes Huck to be an apprentice who has been maltreated by his master, and is running away. The good-hearted, generous lady offers Huck her help; but at the same time she mentions that a reward has been put out for a runaway slave, and she is eager to start looking for him so that she can get the money. What Mrs. Loftus thinks Huck to be, and the actual state of most slaves, are not too far apart- yet while she thinks she is doing the right thing in helping Huck, she has absolutely no qualms about trying to turn Jim in. Something tells me it's not the size of the reward.

But an even more trenchant example comes in the latter half of the book, when Huck is talking to Aunt Sally about a fictitious boat collision. "Anybody hurt?" Aunt Sally asks, to which Huck replies, "No'm. Killed a nigger." Aunt Sally breathes a sigh of relief. "Well, that's good, because sometimes people do get hurt." And this is the wife of a preacher speaking! That lives can really be worth no more than that- the notion nears impossibility. Yet Twain insists on including this appalling exchange. If this isn't to drive home a point, I don't know what it is.

My second argument, that the protagonist is still not fully developed, and that the book follows his development rather than his completed philosophy. When one reads this book it is crucial to remember that *Huck Finn* is a bildungsroman. It traces the psychological and mental development of a young, undeveloped character, and the reader learns the lessons that Huck learns at the same time he does. As young and inexperienced, then, as the narrator is, he is necessarily unreliable. He is more heavily influenced by the social customs than by his own judgments and standards.

Mark Twain does arrange it so that the protagonist has slightly more flexibility than the average youngster. First of all, Huck is an outcast; he has been living on the periphery of society his entire life. This allows Huck to be even younger than he is; he owns a sincere, sweet innocence- almost like that of a baby. Huck thus gains a lot more leeway from the social prejudices of the time. His views of Blacks are not as discriminatory as those of the society. Secondly, Huck has missed a reliable father figure all his life. His own biological father was a chronic alcoholic who gave his son regular beatings and condemned abolition regularly in his drunken rages. This pathetic attempt at a father leaves a big gap which Jim is able to come in through and fill as the first solid, constant older male in Huck's life. Huck's ignorance of social values and his need for a paternal figure is what allows Jim to reasonably enter Huck's life and change his view.

This, too, is what allows the unsatisfactory ending- and the stronger ultimate message that the ending carries. When Tom Sawyer re-enters the scene, Huck again melts back into the landscape, allowing Tom to concoct crazy plans to extract Jim from captivity while passively watching and helping him. Why does he do this? Throughout the book it is obvious that Huck looks up to Tom as a superior. Since Huck is insecure about his very dubious standing in society, Tom, for him, represents a figure that is older and wiser. That Tom is the one who takes control of the situation thus implies that however individuals might change in their views, it will be long before the society can bring itself to accept the right and humanity of slaves, and individuals will not be able to stand up and protest either.

Diction is another part that is highly argued over. This is mainly because of the repetitive use of the word "nigger." As controversial as this word was, Twain had very definite purposes in using it. The first was accurate representation: as of today the word has become the pronoun for all discriminatory, racist epithets. But we do not condemn a mirror from the Bronze Age because the reflection is uneven or coated with patina. Neither do we break it. We respect it for what it is. In the same way we should respect how the people in the past used different tools for the historical information it supplies us, and instead of getting excited and heated up over words that have become inappropriate over the ages, we should learn to accept it as a part of our literary history.

But secondly is the knowledge of the meaning of the word, at least partially. Although it may have been socially common to call Blacks by their offensive epithet, the whites were nonetheless aware that the name was not respectful, to say the least. Margaret Mitchell's *Gone with the Wind* shows us that contrary to popular notion, the word "nigger" carried at least slightly negative connotations even back then. "He had never had the term "nigger" applied to him by a white person in all his life. By other Negroes, yes. But never by a white person⋯ Scarlett felt, rather than saw, the black chin begin to shake with hurt pride, and a killing rage swept over her." (Mitchell, 567) That the use of such an offensive epithet was so rampant subtly underscores the pain that the Blacks had to suffer, working as slaves in harsh conditions.

Even now we still hear comments about racism. When I was in fourth grade a friend sent me a chain email- a protest against the racism still influencing the world today. It seems all so long ago, but when I actually think it through it's not even been a full decade since that happened. But it proves that discrimination is still alive. If not against Blacks, then at least against some other factor of the population, an unheard voice that cries out gently in pain.

And in order for those voices to be heard there needs to be amplifiers, people who will carry those voices and replicate them with louder cries, battering at the mainstream sound. There are many ways to do so. One of them is literature.

Mark Twain was one of the amplifiers of his time. The earnestness with which he carried his social messages continues to make even today a palpable impact on the reader, a vague awe at the clarity and the trenchancy with which he deftly draws his satires. Even all the criticisms that his books receive are signs of his influence- after all, criticisms mean interest.

But back in his time, when this book was still hot off the printing press, it impacted society very palpably, touching people in ways both big and small- a cry for humanity that bounced off insensitive ears and grew louder as these echoes multiplied.

Roman Fever

Introduction

"What will you do this vacation? Though I guess it's pretty obvious, what with that book in your arm."

It was the last day of Mr. Keating's classes for the year, and Selena and I had wandered by his office for a chat. Or, at least, I had-Selena was deeply engaged in conversation with Ms. Lowett, who sat across his desk. Just now I was regretfully thumbing a thick book filled with short stories, purloined from the English library; when teachers were there to check which book you borrowed you didn't always have to check with the librarian, which meant you didn't always have to keep the return date policy. Although I was invariably a speed demon the first time I plowed through a book, good books always enticed me for a second read, a slower drive-through, and often I would have to trot back to the library to renew a particular book that I wanted to reread. I didn't particularly abstain from reading any new books, either, which was probably why I had to renew so often.

"There are so many interesting short stories, but I don't know which ones to read!"

Mr. Keating looked at me with a teasing question on his face, and I nodded eagerly, handing him the book. He motioned for me to pull up Mr. Parry's chair as it was, for the moment, unengaged, and my legs were starting to ache. I gladly obliged.

"Now, let's see. You don't like D. H. Lawrence much-"

"How did you know?"

"Your style. I am your literature teacher, after all. Have you read *The Age of Innocence?*"

"Oh, yes! I loved it!"

Mr. Keating gave me a quiet slanted smile as he pointed to a line of italicized script.

"Well, this story is written by the same author. Maybe you'd like to try it."

I watched Mr. Keating carefully turn down a corner of the page as I smiled, and dared a naughty question.

"I thought you didn't like reading female authors?"

"You make me sound biased! I don't have anything against female authors; I just don't generally like what they write about."

"But Edith Wharton is a woman."

"Well… yes."

We looked at each other and burst out laughing. Mr. Keating handed me the book.

"Here you go, then. Happy reading."

A Tale of Two Women:
Alida and Grace

In *A Tale of Two Cities*, author Charles Dickens used the twin settings of London and Paris, and characters Sydney Carton and Charles Evremonde, in order to juxtapose the conditions within the two countries at that turbulent time period. Likewise, in Edith Wharton's *Roman Fever*, the two protagonists Alida Slade and Grace Ansley narrate their story jointly. The two women, who have lived across each other metaphorically as well as physically their entire lives, represent the two prevalent stereotypes of New York high society in the early twentieth century.

That these women are parallel characters is evident from the very beginning, even in how Wharton uses their appearances to characterize them. Alida Slade is "the lady of high color and energetic brows" (Wharton, 1250), whereas Grace Ansley is "smaller and paler." (Wharton, 1250) The types of compliments Alida received the most often when she was still married was hearing flippant praises of her beauty from the business associates of her husband: "What, that handsome woman with the good clothes and the eyes

is Mrs. Slade- the Slade's wife! Really!" (Wharton, 1252) Grace Ansley
and her own husband, on the other hand, provoke at most highly
respectful responses: "Good-looking, irreproachable, exemplary."
(Wharton, 1252)

The parallelism between the two women is not only apparent
through the differences between their outward appearances but
also through the families they have. Mrs. Slade, who married an
international corporate lawyer, spent her life living in very public
circles and continuously being excited about new, on-the-spur things
to do. Her best recollections of married life comprise of rushing
off on meetings with her husband- "Every day brought its exciting
and unexpected obligation: the impromptu entertaining of eminent
colleagues from abroad, the hurried dashes on legal business to
London, Paris or Rome, where the entertaining was so handsomely
reciprocated." (Wharton, 1252) Conversely, Mr. Ansley is "just the
duplicate of his wife. Museum specimens of New York." (Wharton,
1252) Mrs. Ansley's placid and quiet life is all too boring and pitiful
for busy Mrs. Slade, who launches among her friends a somewhat
barbed joke that she would "rather live opposite a speakeasy for a
change; at least one might see it raided." (Wharton, 1252)

The respective husbands of the two women are not the only ones
that provide foils for the parallel protagonists. Their daughters, too,
serve as their foils, though they serve a slightly different purpose

than the husbands do. It is odd that the very vivacious and vibrant Mrs. Slade would have the meek and angelic Jenny for her daughter; but it is queerer that the daughter of the "museum relics" Barbara Ansley would be the most vivacious character. Mrs. Slade becomes so curious on this part that she even makes so bold as to ask about it- "I was wondering, ever so respectfully, you understand··· wondering how two such exemplary characters as you and Horace had managed to produce anything quite so dynamic." (Wharton, 1255) Since the daughters are thus "reversed", the juxtaposition of the vivacious Babs and the sedate Mrs. Ansley exaggerates the old-school calmness of Mrs. Ansley- and, in the same sense, the calm meditative characteristics of Jenny highlights Mrs. Slade's forgetfulness and insecurity.

What exactly, then, is the relationship between these two protagonists Mrs. Slade and Mrs. Ansley? Neighbors, observers, lifelong acquaintances, yes; but friends? These two ladies "visualize each other, each through the wrong end of her little telescope." (Wharton, 1253) For the reader something strikes wrong the moment the joke about the speakeasy and Mrs. Ansley's house comes out. If Mrs. Slade was truly Mrs. Ansley's friend, it seems that she wouldn't have been quite so eager to demean Mrs. Ansley's circumstances, especially not in the way Mrs. Slade does- like a cat scratching at a rival. Later, Wharton ironically describes the tension running between the two, saying "Like many intimate friends, the two ladies had never before had occasion to be silent together, and Mrs. Ansley was slightly embarrassed by what seemed, after so many years, a new stage in their intimacy, and one with which she did not know how to deal." (Wharton, 1253) From all of Wharton's hints, it is evident that while the two ladies publish themselves as friends, the reality is something less quite so pure of heart.

The struggle between the two women subtly escalates with the flow of the story, peaking as the subject of Roman Fever enters the conversation. Mrs. Slade, goaded into anger by the calmness with which Mrs. Ansley faces the Roman scenery and the memory of the years past, tells Mrs. Ansley out of spite the truth that happened so many years ago in Rome, when both of the girls were being courted. Mrs. Ansley, however, refuses to lose her calm and stays placid, showing only pity for Mrs. Slade. This pity breaks Mrs. Slade more than she can admit.

Admittedly the fight that Mrs. Slade is fighting against Mrs. Ansley is rather one-sided, since Mrs. Ansley is having too hard of a time coping with her own emotions to fight Mrs. Slade back. When Mrs. Ansley first hears Mrs. Slade's confession- that Mrs. Slade forged Mr. Slade's love-note to Mrs. Ansley, and that Mr. Slade had not meant to write it- she freezes for a while, repeating "It was the only letter I ever had from him!" (Wharton, 1257) Soon, however, she regains her

Old New York-like composure and tells Mrs. Slade she feels sorry for her.

And now the question boils down to why Mrs. Slade bothered telling Mrs. Ansley about the incident at the Colosseum, so long after the real incident itself was completed and over. If Alida Slade was trying to pain Mrs. Ansley, then the only success came in the first few minutes of the interaction. Mrs. Slade knew Mrs. Ansley well enough to realize that she would have tight control over her emotions, and that she would not be able to take sufficient pleasure in it. What, then, was the purpose behind Mrs. Slade's confession?

It is likely that Mrs. Slade never had chance to enjoy any true pleasures with her husband. Although she remained his faithful wife until his death, the things she misses most about being Mr. Slade's wife are the material recognition parts, not the spiritually strengthening parts. Being unable to gain that part of Mr. Slade's heart for herself, knowing that any other girl might have once had access to it would break Mrs. Slade's identity completely. By making Grace Ansley just another failed part of Mr. Slade's one-shot flirt, Mrs. Slade gains, at least mentally, a certain stabilizing dominance over both Grace Ansley and Mr. Slade.

Until now, having never talked to Mrs. Ansley about what she truly felt for Mr. Slade, and only having had a vague fear that Mr. Slade might have liked the sweeter Mrs. Ansley better than herself, Mrs.

Slade had only a sense of jealousy of Mrs. Ansley to battle with. After thinking what a good prospective match Mrs. Ansley's daughter Babs will land, and spitefully thinking how her own daughter Jenny won't manage anything, Mrs. Slade repentantly thinks, "there was no one of whom she had less right to think unkindly than of Grace Ansley. Would she never cure herself of envying her! Perhaps she had begun too long ago." (Wharton, 1255)

In realizing that the emotions between Mr. Slade and Mrs. Ansley ran deeper than she even suspected, however, Mrs. Slade destroys that part of herself that was longing so badly for some type of control over a part of her life that she could not have control over- namely, Delphin's love. This, indeed, was the Roman Fever that Mrs. Ansley's great-aunts suffered from, and used to use as a means to keep unruly children indoors. In love with a man that they could not control and would not reciprocate their loves, the great-aunts, according to the story at least, go mad. This draws a striking parallel to Mrs. Ansley's own choice when she was young and in love with Delphin Slade; how she crept out in the middle of the night to the Colosseum, no matter what the consequences were. In the eyes of the public, who knew nothing of the true father of the child Babs, Mrs. Ansley was the failed one. And because Mrs. Slade was the successful one who could not be sure of her success, the story of the Roman fever came back to haunt her over and over again, possibly for the rest of her life.

Roman Fever is an excellently written, powerful short story by Edith Wharton. The issues are dealt with surprising clarity and organization of emotion, and the twist at the end of the story affords an agreeable surprise to all readers. Emotions of love, jealousy, triumph, defeat, gain, and loss, are all touchingly portrayed in this story, strengthened by the parallel characters whose walk along two parallel lengths of road makes their paths unpredictable!

The Age of Innocence

Of Innocence and Deception

It is ironical that whereas love has been commercialized to the point of becoming a banality in today's society, this trend has conversely driven us farther away from the fundamental topic of *true* love, and it has become increasingly difficult to find love described in literature as it is found in reality.

Think about it: the thousand-and-one prototypes of unbelievable and cliched turns of events, the princesses who all manage to fall in love at first sight and live happily ever after, the ardent lover with the rose clenched in his teeth and the lady who turns coquettishly away from him; vampires created solely for the purpose of pleasure, tolerated for the sensual flights of fancy they afford the reader. All of this is rather hilarious in a horrific sense: horrific, since the very universality of this superficial image of love is what the society promotes and thus must be what the society deems desirable.

But even so the truth manages to surface, from time to time, eluding the overbearing umbrella of soulless fantasies. I am reminded of the recently released Disney movie *Frozen*, which was lauded for its characters and its plot. The princesses were necessarily princesses, Disney being Disney, but they managed to retain a persona different from the rest of the Disney princess company. Elsa might be cold and frigid, but her well-guarded heart contains depth beyond what most people can imagine. Ana is clumsy, bold, outrageous, and utterly adorable; she depends not on men but on her own integrity and daring. In many ways it is a much-needed redefinition and purification of old ideals and a true representation of the new ones: the woman of today stands by herself, independent and strong, and much to the sorrow of Oscar Wilde[2] her first love is rarely her last. The songs and the banter might be playful and comedic, but the social reprimand remains evident.

Elsa and Ana remind me of a woman in a book that I love very much. The woman, like Ana, is bold and daring and unconventional; like Elsa, she has an almost incalculable depth of heart. She plays a crucial role in spinning out one of the greatest romances in print, and in criticizing the superficiality of the society by which she is surrounded. The woman is Ellen Olenska, and the book is *The Age of Innocence*.

When we read about extramarital affairs, we cannot help but read with a prejudiced eye. When I was a sophomore, it was the

2) Irish author and playwright. In his play *A Woman of No Importance*, Wilde wrote, "Men always want to be a woman's first love. That is there clumsy vanity. We women have a more subtle instinct about things. What we like is to be a man's last romance."

popular trend to seem as to read entirely without discrimination; but it must be admitted that the trend succeeded in only bringing about the *appearance* of reading without discrimination- without any actual change of heart. For my many friends who might flare up at my generalization, please remember: we sigh when we read of the dashing dreaming husband whose life is dragged down by the weight of his duller wife, and sometimes we even are inspired to encourage his infidelity- after all, he's a hopeless romantic, and he won't be persuaded to believe that beauty is entirely out of his reach. *But none of us would willingly trade places with the wife.* Or, if you are a boy, perhaps it would be easier to imagine a charming woman whose caprice and passion cannot be sated by her plebian husband, that we are trying to justify. Either case works. The truth is that the prejudice cannot be eliminated.

And it is entirely right that this prejudice should stay. However liberal society might progress on to become, the keystones of society should necessarily remain stagnant. Marriage is one such keystone: it lies on the fundaments of commitment and loyalty, and on the fundamental belief that we hold these values to be beautiful. Affairs, then, cannot help but be a sacrilege to this world. Recall Gustave Flaubert's *Madam Bovary.* We might sympathize with poor Emma, but our pity does not reach the point of justification. I am sure the reader will agree on the reprehensibility of the relationships Emma seeks.

The Age of Innocence, however, should be excluded from this category. *Age* also deals with an engaged man's love for a married woman, and the relationship between Newland Archer and Ellen Olenska seems much like any other clandestine affair at first glance. Because of the love that they share, the duties that they own to their real partners go neglected. What differentiates their relationship, then, from those of others, is the keen muteness of the social background that surrounds their love.

Newland Archer's world lies primarily in the tightly regulated sphere of New York high-class society, where the verdict on fashion and propriety and graceful indolence play "a part as important in Newland Archer's New York as the inscrutable totem terrors that had ruled the destinies of his forefathers thousands of years ago." (Wharton, 2) His primary joy is in being one of the most socially correct young men of New York and newly accepted fiance of the graceful May Welland, and his happiest fantasies are of educating her from utter naivete to social completion by teaching her to appreciate great literary works and historical legacy.

It is into this world that Madam Olenska, the unhappy countess, arrives. Although she has been New York-bred from young she has been away too long to remember the gravity that the trivial etiquette demands carries in the society, and has experienced too much of importance to consider them important. The unintentional flippancy with which she deftly condemns the society startles and even insults Archer in the beginning, but slowly it hones his eye to the deficiencies in the fundamental superficiality of New York. Starting from the moment he starts defending Madam Olenska Archer realizes that his fiance May is not as naive, but instead "only an artificial product··· [a] creation of factitious purity, so cunningly manufactured by a conspiracy of mothers and aunts and grandmothers and long-dead ancestresses." (Wharton, 36) From then on, the widening of his horizon continues in leaps and bounds: some time later, at a party comprised primarily of elderly women he notes that their eyes "struck him as curiously immature compared with hers [Madam Olenska's]. It frightened him to think what must have gone to the making of her eyes." (Wharton, 50)

Next to such depth the beauty of the skin-deep, or the grace comprised of calculations, cannot help but diminish. Archer gradually finds himself falling in love with the charming Madam Olenska, whose appreciation of beauty and truth is as keen as his own. They converse at a level wholly unimaginable in an exchange between Archer and May. Their interactions have power in their purpose and meaning.

It is ironic to note here that the reason Archer first really noticed Ellen was due to the fact that her near-divorced presence acted as a sort of blemish on the Mingotts, her maiden family. Since Archer was to marry into this family he considered it his duty to protect the honor of the Mingotts as well as the reputation of many who shared the same name, and he decided the reputation would be helped significantly if two of New York's oldest and best established families were to publicize their support of Madame Olenska. In the course of conversing with Ellen, however, he himself comes to feel the utter authoritarian dictatorship of the Family as a true dictatorship, and to lament its scrupulous attention to trivialities- despite the fact that it is this very power that brought him to open his eyes. "She [May] paused, embarrassed and yet smiling, and Archer suddenly saw before him the embodied image of the Family⋯ [he stared] with unseeing eyes at the list of guests that she had put in his hand." (Wharton, 285)

But the irony underlying Archer and Ellen's relationship allows their love to become pure and poignant- their love never degrades into the physical. As frustrated as the reader becomes at Archer's original New York, the relationship that Archer and Ellen have remains the only sensible yet the only fantastic thing, the only thing that appreciates truth and beauty for being truth and beauty. The love is as important symbolically to the book as it is for the realities of Archer and Ellen. Therefore, the moment the love shows even remote hints of degrading into vulgar passions as shared by the rest of society, it is right that the affair disintegrates and is discontinued. The poignancy and the pain and the regret that the reader feels in Archer's place is an implicit condemnation of the stifling society that created such heartburn.

On the whole Wharton does a scintillating job of drawing out New York society subtly as a site of outrageous condemnation, but there is one point that seems logically inconsistent. Most of the people that are introduced in the book are short-thought and inextricably tied to the codes of society that act as their law as well as the determining standard of the social grace of the day. These New Yorkers have largely been York-born and York-bred, and this scrupulous attention to fashion and details has always been a part of their life.

Madam Olenska is different from the average person. She was adopted into New York society when she was a young girl and sent back out when she married into Polish nobility, and she has seen much of the world- much more than just the limited, confined sphere of polished New York. When Archer introduces Ellen, saying that "she doesn't care a hang about where she lives- or about any of our little social sign-posts," his reporter friend Ned remarks, "Hmm- been in bigger places, I suppose." (Wharton, 103) Thus it is logical that Ellen's horizon is double the scope of that of any other woman: she has learned to take society at its true value, refusing to imbue it with more worth than what it merits.

But Newland Archer's implausibility somewhat undermines Wharton's credibility. Archer is from a very old, very well-known family in New York; his cousins, the Van der Luydens, are the leaders of New York society, and the very embodiments of etiquette. His concordance to their social customs reveals itself in Wharton's wry reference to "the duty of using two silverbacked brushes with his monogram in blue enamel to part his hair, and of never appearing in society without a flower (preferably a gardenia) in his buttonhole." (Wharton, 2)

But soon his horizon has become as lofty as that of Ellen's, although the spheres in which Archer and Ellen have spent the bulk of their lives are widely different. Archer does admit that he has seen much less pain than Ellen, who has "had to look at the eyes of the Gorgon," (Wharton, 245) but still there is not much difference in how the two lovers determine what is beautiful or not. The inconsistency lies in how Archer can recognize this beauty. There is nothing in Archer's provincial life that suggests knowledge of true beauty, nor anything that could have inspired a sense of it. And this sense is not something that can be manufactured or made at the spur of the moment. It must have been instilled with patience and a continuous supreme appreciation for the finer emotions of life. Archer, though he is admirable, is forced and unreal in the very thing that makes him admirable.

Disregarding the minor discrepancy regarding Archer, however, *The Age of Innocence* is a wonderful book, keen and socially piercing. The focus of illicit love is touching and poignant since it is not love written for the sake of the sense of love, but for the sake of the criticism of the society. The resulting cleanness of the love is what makes it beautiful and entices the reader for a second read. It brings out the social criticism to a sparkling point of invisible finesse and adroitness which rivals cannot hope to compete with. Even Fitzgerald could not hope for victory if he were to be pitted against such an opponent.

Once, when I was writing a timed essay, I called a certain woman author a "female Fitzgerald." I believe it was actually Edith Wharton herself that I was writing about. Generally teachers don't approve of such generalizations in AP essays, and that was what we were training for at the time, so I got points docked for the comment, but then- and even now- the only thing I regret was that I feel I gave Edith Wharton an insufficient epithet. Wharton's keen summarization of society, apparent through her sensitive rendering of the New York life, should elevate her status, so that she remains no longer a "female Fitzgerald", but instead so that Fitzgerald becomes known as a "male Wharton."

Part Two

Life on Stage

: Plays

The Importance of Being Earnest

Introduction

In the Norton Reader for English Literature, a thick volume with wafer-thin pages scribed with glorious literary works, is a play titled *The Importance of Being Earnest*. It is one of my favorite plays.

I always had a vague fascination with the Norton Reader. It was my aunt's textbook once, when she was in college. The various notes she had taken on the margin, though now faded and ineligible, had always seemed to me like a magic formula that could transport me back in time to whatever world the piece of literature was talking about- if read with the right intonation. I had started playing with the book when I was in sixth grade, flipping through the pages first for the sheer pleasure of hearing those silky sheets collide and slide together, than for the actual content itself. In seventh grade I skimmed through some of the shorter stories; in eighth grade I perused my first play- *The Importance of Being Earnest*.

I remember I was so impressed with the play that I started recommending it to fellow book-lovers. One of them was my sister. She was a senior at the time and very busy, but she made time one

Sunday afternoon to read the play.

"What did you think of it?"

"Do the characters even know what they're talking about?"

My sister's disgusted reply left me smirking. She was a stickler for rules and exactness, even back then, and she preferred literary works where people knew exactly what they meant to say and meant exactly what they said.

But my sister's response did nothing to alter my love for Oscar Wilde's nonsense- if anything, it heightened my hunger for his works. By the time I was a sophomore I had already worked my way through a volume of Wilde's plays with Jaemin. It was his book that we were reading. When I left Korea he gave me the book, knowing how much I had loved the plays, and he signed it "from Jaemin, who will always remember the Wilde times we had."

It's impossible not to have wild laughs when you're reading Wilde's works.

An Earnest Analysis of the Importance of Being Earnest

"On the contrary, Aunt Augusta, I've now realized for the first time

in my life the vital Importance of Being Earnest."

- Jack, *The Importance of Being Earnest*

Of the many humorists and satirists that have put pen to paper to record their thoughts, there have not been many as scintillating as Oscar Wilde.

Having read and enjoyed Wilde's plays, both by myself and with fellow literature-loving peers, I have come to the conclusion that Wilde's plays can generally be read on two levels. The first level is what might be called the first-time-through interpretation, and its primary achievement is that it captivates the readers by Wilde's sparkling wit, his incandescent repartees, and his skilfully sketched caricatures.

The thirst for the second level is what brings readers back time and again, helpless in the powerful grasp of Wilde's writing. The social message he seeks to deliver, and the social context in which he wrote, both significantly influence the way in which his works may be interpreted. The readers might howl with laughter at Wilde's wit, but what draws them is the whole new world that lies beyond the world as seen through the naked eye.

The second day of my sophomore Literature class, Mr. Keating taught us that it was important not to let the author's personal history over-influence our literary interpretations. It was an immensely interesting, edifying class that would leave a deeply scored mark on how I viewed literature.

The way Mr. Keating went about his goal was this: he had us read Arthur Rimbaud's *A Winter's Dream* and analyze it, in groups, but to each group he gave a different hint about the author. One group thought Rimbaud was Communist. Another group heard that he was Black. By the time that all the groups had covertly managed to share what their clue was- Mr. Keating had warned us not to share our clues- Rimbaud had become a Black Communist homosexual woman who liked eating something. I believe it was either cotton candies or bananas, but I can't be too sure. Mr. Keating heard our muted grumbling at the statistical chances of a writer being all that at once, and he cracked up.

"This is why you don't do what the teacher tells you not to do," he assured us.

After we found out that none of the clues about Rimbaud were true, except for the fact that he was homosexual, the entire class turned on Mr. Keating like cats spitting fire. For most of us, the clues had rendered our analyses useless. Laughing, he held up his hands against our onslaught.

"Well, now you know. The author's life isn't always tied to his work."

When I was analyzing Wilde's works with Jaemin, I hesitantly mentioned this episode. He stared at me almost as if he thought I was crazy.

"Are you crazy?"

Okay, so he really thought I was crazy.

"You can't analyze a piece of satire without knowing what's being satirized. Wilde's entire life was lived on the Victorian stage, and it's just about the only thing he knows how to satirize! Knowing his background and his literary movement is crucial!"

I think I did well to submit to Jaemin's judgment. He was right. After a little background research on Wilde, his works came under an entirely new light. It was an exhilarating experience- like getting glasses for the very first time: seeing something faintly, the outlines blurred, at first; and then realizing that one needed glasses, getting them, then seeing the same thing again with lines of almost shocking clarity. While it's definitely important not to tie analyses based entirely on the lives of authors, it is doubly important to know information crucial to the analyzing procedure- and know it well.

Wilde was a famous pioneer of aestheticism and believed that the artist should incorporate more beauty into art, assisting with the movement to replace the utilitarian ideals of the time with the more immediate ideals of beauty and pleasure. He had a sincere dislike of the social codes and prejudices of high Victorian society, but his works focused heavily on mocking its delicate, well-bred, modest beauty without distorting the truth. His social comedies, as they came to be known, were welcomed with open arms, though some of the conservative critics were indisposed towards them. These plays, all of which were immensely popular, included *An Ideal Husband, A Woman of No Importance, Lady Windermere's Fan,* and *The Importance of Being Earnest.*

It is interesting how Wilde managed to so completely win over the public. Not many people would enjoy seeing their own society condensed into stereotypes on stage and ridiculed- indeed, it is seldom enjoyed even in today's more open-minded society. How, then, did Wilde accomplish this superhuman feat? Let us inspect Wilde's most famous play, *The Importance of Being Earnest*, for clues.

In *Importance*, Wilde's gentle mockery reaches its peak. Despite the fact that it only has eight characters and figures four prominently, it nonetheless manages to draw Victorian society with a few brilliant strokes. As the double meaning behind the very title suggests, the play centers on the importance of honesty and names- or rather, the lack of it.

The lightness of the characters is crucial for the accurate communication of the play's meaning. Algernon, Jack, Cecily, and Gwendolen, though they are all rather flat and one-sided, have an irresistible allure. The gravity with which they give their inane speeches endows them with an enchanting stupidity. They are like bright pieces of blown glass, dyed different colors, which in the light give off a multicolored shine distorted by the smooth helix of the surface, and which have nothing but an air pocket under that fine play of evanescent colors on the surface. Cecily and Gwendolen might very well be the precursors of the alluring but hollow girls of S. Fitzgerald's Jazz Age: breathy with youth and excitement and empty-headed pleasure, and captivated by the ideals that they themselves create. Algernon and Jack are as thoughtless as the girls are, heartily willing to go along with the fools' play as long as it will get them the wife they respectively desire. They actually don't even feel it to be a fools' play. Bunburying, as Algernon says, is an art; and the dolls' tea party is as much of a serious life-and-death matter for them as it is for seven-year-old girls who are supposed to play at it.

That Cecily and Gwendolen, the representative stand-ins for the Victorian society, place such an importance on the name Earnest is ironic. First of all, that the girls would consider it a "girlish dream of mine to love a man named Earnest" shows how trivialized love is. Shakespeare's quote, "What's in a name?" finds its true worth in this play. A name means nothing but an outward cover, a reference to the person who owns it. Victorian society is captivated by this outward appearance of people: it doesn't care what happens secretly, behind the scenes; all it cares for is propriety and correctness on the outside.

Secondly, the name Earnest is ironic, since the characters here are anything but earnest. Everyone participates in deceit, considering it necessary to survive in society. This is a continually recurring theme in the book. Lady Bracknell, who represents the older counterpart of Victorian society and thus symbolizes the set mores of the time, mentions when she speaks of her husband, "I do not propose to undeceive him. Indeed, I have never undeceived him on any question. I would consider it wrong." When she is talking to Cecily, she says, "Indeed, no woman should ever be quite accurate about her age. It looks so calculating."

But the deceit does not end with only Lady Bracknell, or the older generations. When Jack realizes that his Christian name is truly Earnest, he apologizes to Gwendolen, saying, "It is a terrible thing for a man to find out suddenly that all his life he has been speaking nothing but the truth. Can you forgive me?" Even more shockingly, Gwendolen replies, "I can. For I feel that you are sure to change." As lightly and inanely as this may have been written, it is still a biting attack of the hypocrisy rampant in Victorian society, both old and young. The people claim to cling onto Christian ideals, but in truth, deceit is so rampant as to seem a necessary ingredient of both domestic and social life.

Wilde's audience was, for the most part, keen and well-educated. Undoubtedly Wilde's sarcasm and his titular irony would not have gone unnoticed. Yet Wilde remained well-loved in the very society he was attacking. This was in due thanks to the characters. Firstly, as stupid and shallow as they may seem, the characters that Wilde creates are nonetheless cheerful and enchanting. As I wrote earlier, they are like pieces of blown glass in a way- and they are also like butterflies: they are fragile, weak, impractical, and not good for much else except for flying around from flower to flower looking beautiful, but for their very iridescence and delicacy the watcher is drawn towards them. Wilde's world of beautiful characters allows the audience not only to love them, and thus the play, but also to view the whole of Victorian society with a more forgiving eye.

The second factor lies in the fact that the characters are only children playing in an adult form. Their faults come from an ignorance that cannot be blamed, but only loved, and corrected in due time. We abhor lying in a gentleman of fifty years of age, but in a little boy of five the lie is adorable, cute, and something that must be corrected for sake of his future, so that he does not develop into the gentleman at fifty. Algernon, Jack, Cecily, and Gwendolen are all such childish versions of the real Victorian society. Thus while the audience would have realized all too clearly the criticism Wilde was trying to get across, they would also have appreciated Wilde's efforts to make the criticism palatable.

Wilde's writing is undeniably impressive. By mixing the right amounts of his glittering wit along with his heavy sarcasm, Wilde renders his plays not merely endurable but instead enjoyable, almost luxurious, to the audience that he criticizes. While his social criticism may not be as clear in his plays due to the charming qualities of his effervescent characters, his message is definitely all the more clearer for the gentle taste it leaves in one's mouth. Wilde's approach would be commendable, even from the viewpoint of any leader seeking to improve the society he leads. And after all, literature is not only the benchmark and reporter, but also the initiator and the leader of a society.

An Ideal Husband

The Age of Ideals

When Jaemin was reading *An Ideal Husband* with me, we had a lot of fun- even more than the fun we had reading *The Importance of Being Earnest*.

It wasn't because of the characters, necessarily, or the plot; no other play of Wilde's is quite as lighthearted or as frivolous as *Importance*, though *Ideal* is satisfyingly laughable. The fun behind this work lies in the questions that the readers are forced to ask themselves throughout the play. What is this play trying to say? Does the playwright do a good job of communicating his message? How are we supposed to deal with the incongruities that the author doesn't bother clarifying?

The real reason Jaemin and I liked this play so much was because it was one of the few pieces of literature that we felt comfortable dissing. Don't get us wrong; I doubt either of us could ever scare up a work like this. But in literature class the students were often required to analyze a piece of work, and more often than not criticize it, and it was those assignments that were the most painful.

What if we thought Mark Twain was a wonderful writer and that the rough, unpolished character of Huckleberry Finn left nothing to be desired? What if we thought that Shakespeare's use of slapstick in *Romeo and Juliet* was hilarious and added a sense of much-needed comic relief? How were we supposed to criticize authors of books in which we could see no flaw?

The reason, then, that Jaemin and I jumped at the chance to criticize Wilde's work for once, was mainly because both of us had respectively finished a most grueling exercise- Mr. Henderson wanted a criticism on *The Catcher in the Rye*, and Mr. Keating had ordered him to write a similar paper on Kurt Vonnegut's *Slaughterhouse-Five*. Needless to say, Jaemin and I were dying. We both loved the books that we were supposed to be criticizing- well, actually, I loved mine, Jaemin might have hated his- and it was just so plain dang hard to find any faults. It generally wasn't too hard to see why the author might have used this particular device in order to convey this exact idea, or to praise how sophisticatedly he had used a certain vehicle, so that his message might be delivered all the clearer. But it was completely different, and completely difficult, to note how insufficient some pieces of work were, or to think up of new venues through which the author might improve his work. Although Jaemin and I had protested at the time, Mr. Henderson had been accurate in his assessment that we were too much on the passive side of the reading scale.

The reason we started reading Wilde's plays was not, actually, for active reading practice, but because they were funny and we thought they would help us blow off stress. We were fully expecting to like *The Importance of Being Earnest* best since we both had read the play beforehand and knew how terribly funny it was. It was only after we read *An Ideal Husband* that we realized what a glorious amount could be corrected there, and from then on it became the best work of the plays.

I don't think it's anything to do with being fundamentally wicked, even though that's what Mr. Henderson accused Jaemin and me of being when he overheard us criticize *Ideal* with such relish. Though I really quite suspect we are fundamentally wicked. Considering the delight with which we tore apart *Ideal*, it's very likely. But there's a certain euphoria that comes with being able to criticize a literary giant for once. It proves that they have their human moments. It gives us hope that we fledglings might, one day, be able to reach that status, and make as few lapses into human faults as they have made.

Ideal focuses largely on two topics which still take up a good deal of society's attention, even today- firstly, the importance of honesty; and secondly, politics. It was easier for Jaemin to criticize the second topic, since he was aiming to major in International Relations anyways, and while we were eating dinner he gave me a round analysis of why Mrs. Cheveley and Sir Robert were both to blame, strictly politically speaking, and how the reader should not be really compelled to stand only on Sir Robert's side and condemn Mrs. Cheveley.

We had expected to debate, or at least fall into friendly wrangling over a part of an analysis, since our analyses rarely coincided. It wasn't often that we would make similar conclusions, even when we were dealing with the same topic. So I was planning to organize everything that I had thought out while listening to Jaemin's analysis, as people often do in debates, but his trenchant acuity surprised me so much that I was actually unable to do anything of the sort. He had organized the thoughts in my brain that I had not been able to sift yet from the fluff. Jaemin's analysis surprisingly coincided largely with my own, even though I had left politics entirely to him and had only focused on the first issue of honesty. We had come across one of those moments of rarity: moments when our conclusions coincided- in this case, that Sir Robert and Mrs. Cheveley were equally to blame.

Mrs. Cheveley is a charming woman, "making great demands on one's curiosity." She is graceful, womanly, attractive- and she hides a viper's fangs behind her sweet feminine self. She is clever and she knows how to manipulate the truth. For her, the adage "truth is power" has more importance than any other, since it is with her beauty and the hidden truths she knows that she has made her place and her fortune. While she acknowledges and embraces her hidden pasts and scandals, she holds necessary deceptions close around her in order that she might maintain her position in society.

But Mrs. Cheveley is not the only character to be so deceptive. Sir Robert is one of the greatest actors to appear on stage. His initial appearance is that of the model husband, the paragon of goodness. He is perfect, ideal, godlike; we do not see any faults in him, until Mrs. Cheveley draws out his faults in her conversation. It is only then that we see the man of clay behind the marble statue. Sir Robert is as susceptible to bribes and temptations as the rest of humanity. Having once fallen, however, Sir Robert tries to cover it up, and pretend it never happened. He disguises his faults and his shortcomings with lies and a facade of perfection. The marble statue is made from lies.

Why is Sir Robert, then, so much more engaging than Mrs. Cheveley? The difference lies in how they view themselves- or rather, how they lie to themselves. Sir Robert captivates our admiration because he excellently carries on the pretense of believing in his own righteousness. Whether he really believes so, is rather arbitrary. In many ways it seems as if Sir Robert is deceiving himself in order to live without feeling too much guilt. At other times it seems like he feels no guilt at all, since in the past, he has already managed to soothe himself saying that it was all for the better and a very necessary step. He has tried to sell off his conscience, by giving large amounts of money to charitable organizations, and by pushing away the past and pretending it doesn't exist he has managed to be liberated from the pangs of guilt.

It is interesting that in yet another way, Mrs. Cheveley is more honest than Sir Robert. She does not mince words about how she brought about her own fortune; she does not cringe at what she has done, but neither does she deny it. To Mrs. Cheveley, at least, truth is an unfortunate medicine that must be swallowed at all costs to gain wealth and power, and she will use it as well as ignore it depending on the circumstances.

Mrs. Cheveley's hard heart, and how easily she faces and manipulates the truth, is what decisively turns the reader against her. When the reader faces Sir Robert, they face a man who is unwilling to remember the wrongs he has done, a man who is trying to push it far behind himself, and they see the vestiges of a once-good man in him, albeit a man who is tired of being haunted by the past. The very fact that he has been so successful in pushing the past behind him and carrying on an excellent pretense of believing in his own righteousness, hints at the amounts of struggles Sir Robert must have already gone through in order to compromise with his originally high moral standards. In such cases it is all too easy for the man to lower his moral standards, but Sir Robert keeps them as they originally were. More work, yes; but Sir Robert is more than willing to do more work in order to remain faithful to at least a part of his integrity. He is willing to work with himself so that he can find a point of justifiability in his wrongs, and continue to keep his moral standards without feeling like a hypocrite.

When the reader sees Mrs. Cheveley, however, they see a cold, calculating woman. She is admittedly more brutally honest than Sir Robert in some ways, but her conscience has been hardened to the point that no amount of painful or dishonorable truth can shame her any more. Truth is no longer something that she either despises or treasures- it is no longer a value of any worth. It is a weapon, an ornamentation which she wears as easily as her dangerous beauty. If Mrs. Cheveley was not such a villain from the womb, then she definitely is one of those contemptible, despicable characters who loosen their moral standards after having committed the first wrong- the type of man Sir Robert is so honorable for not being.

Since the story concludes so, with Sir Robert lauded as the superior character and Mrs. Cheveley as the inferior one, it must be that Sir Robert ends happily, while Mrs. Cheveley does not. But the question remains: does Sir Robert deserve his happiness? He has not been punished for his faults in the past, except for perhaps two days of breathtaking worry. With this, is his punishment about to end? Something in the world of justice does not seem right. Jaemin and I agreed that Wilde's *Ideal* found its fundamental fault in this point.

As a last point of interest, it is interesting to note who Wilde establishes as the titular character, a question that is actually unsolved until the end of the play. Like all of Wilde's society plays, the social message is again directed towards the Victorian audience, and the point of criticism is the ideals that the Victorians hold. Sometimes they pressure a man beyond breaking, because as in *Ideal*, a man has to push away his past and deny it. He has no place in which he can be entirely weak and human. The marble pedestal on which ideals are placed and worshipped becomes tiringly stiff and narrow, especially for the guilt-ridden man, and the ideals on the pedestals wobble, unable to keep their balance, and come dangerously close to falling over and shattering into a thousand shards.

Initially, for the reader, it is a surprise that Lord Goring would be published as the conclusively ideal husband here. With his strict attentions to vanity and gracefulness and pleasure, and in stark contrast against the strict forward-thinking politician Sir Robert, Lord Goring would probably be the last candidate for an ideal. What does a dandy accomplish, other than being charming and ornamental? Nothing.

Lord Caversham, Goring's father, threatens Goring that unless he makes Mabel an ideal husband, he will "cut you [Goring] off with a shilling," and Mabel replies that she doesn't want a perfect husband, but that she wants to be a "real wife" to Goring. Goring, himself, says nothing. But Wilde was wise in establishing Goring as the desirably ideal husband. Even for the audience, who has spent the duration of the play watching how nearly Sir Robert and Lady Chiltern's marriage comes to failure, the ideal of the husband would have become altered to one who has a real wife, a wife who loves him without being mistaken about any ideals. And after watching the near-demise of Sir Robert's character, the audience tires of hearing of perfect people. They come to desire people who are polished, well-made, scrupulously attentive to goodness, givers of warmth and sound advice, and careless of sensible advice. Lord Goring, Wilde's stand-in character, becomes the last star. Farewell to Victorian prudery. Aestheticism rules.

It's just another last attack on the Victorian society of ideals.

Lady Windermere's Fan and A Woman of No Importance

Misanthropy in Wilde's Works

"A misanthrope I can understand- a woman-thrope, never!"

- Miss Prism, *The Importance of Being Earnest*

Although today Wilde is most famous for the utmost beauty of the language that his characters speak, in his time he was renowned for his unconventional plays and the effect they evoked from society.

The era during which Wilde lived was a time that was still heavily ruled by Victorian standards. As George Bernard Shaw's works more than amply show, it was a time when women were beginning to realize their own worth and be proud of the wages that they were making from their work, instead of thinking it a shame. But that was for the rising middle-class. On the higher tiers of society women were still innocent things, perhaps clever, but still fragile; things that had to be protected and carefully shielded from any of the real issues of life, which the men would characteristically take it upon themselves to discuss.

Wilde was a critic of the Victorian society and its stifling and sometimes self-contradictory conduct, and if he initially had no proponents he forged them with his tremendous will and wit. Even today his social plays remain masterpieces, a legacy of one of the most trenchant authors of the nineteenth century.

This admirable playwright left two plays discussing the women of these Victorian times, and it is these two plays that I propose to inspect today: *Lady Windermere's Fan* (hence *Lady*), *and A Woman of No Importance* (hence *Woman*). Both plays deal with the classic "fallen woman" of Victorian society. But as befits plays criticizing the incongruence of the era's social beliefs, the women are painted in much softer lights, in kinder lines, and the reflection from the mirror of literature that glares back at them is softer and kinder yet. *Lady* deals with a woman's struggle to decide between an unloving husband and an eager lover. *Woman* deals with an internal battle between a woman's conflicting desires: to keep her son, or to give him to his immoral, illegitimate father.

While Wilde sought to remove the pretentiousness of Victorian manners from society by satirizing them in his plays, it is still of worth to note that the general society as portrayed in the play was unaware that either of the women was depraved. It was a necessary setting in order for the play firstly to gain credibility and secondly to communicate its message. Firstly, judging by the ruling social beliefs of the time, no "nice" woman would ever talk to such personifications of depravity, and in order for these "nice" women to be criticized they needed to at least be on speaking terms with the subject matter. Secondly, the fact that these "nice" women thought the supposedly "bad" women to be the paragon of modesty, as they do in *Woman*, is an irony that drives Wilde's message home: the bad woman is only what society makes out to be as the bad woman. And in these plays seeking to reconstruct the social perception of "fallen women" the reader notes an interesting trend: a slight leaning towards women's rights, and hints of how they should be viewed equally to men.

So now, having established the rudiments of each play, let us inspect what led the women of both plays to be led astray. In *Lady*, a woman suffers from the misunderstanding that her husband is seeing a mistress- in truth, her mother. She is tempted to run away with a lover, but her mother comes and stops her from doing so. In *Woman*, a young man is offered an excellent job position by his illegitimate father. The man's mother does not want to let the father take the son, and at the end she admits the truth to her son, who has grown enough in moral strength to be able to spurn the father's offer and step away.

For *Lady*, objectively speaking, the blame lies equally on both parts- both Lady and Lord Windermere are in the wrong. The initial wrong was with Lord Windermere. He should have loved and respected his wife enough to tell her that he was seeing Lady Windermere's mother. While Lord Windermere's show of consideration for his wife is sweet, it shows want of true thoughtfulness and attention.

And it seems that Wilde was also aiming to implicitly criticize, at the same time, the Victorian view of the paragon of women: as sweet, dumb little dolls that do not have the capacity to understand human affairs. If Lord Windermere had appreciated his wife's capacity for intelligence and strength, and confided in her, this play could have never existed. We have no way of knowing if Wilde had a secret sympathy for women's rights, but his conviction of the intelligence of women seems to suggest it.

But Lord Windermere should not be the only one to have to take the blame. Lady Windermere, also, should not have jumped to the conclusion that her husband was seeing a mistress. Simultaneously, while jealousy is an emotion that nearly everyone who has engaged in a romantic relationship will understand, Lady Windermere's judgment also has scope to be considered rash. The importance of trust in a relationship remains unchanged today, even in a world where everything- including people and bonds linking them- passes by much quicker.

The driving hero of the plot, thankfully, is neither Lady nor Lord Windermere, but the mother, Mrs. Erlynne. We never know exactly what happened to her. We can only guess that it is something similar to the rift between Lord and Lady Windermere that happened to Mrs. Erlynne and her husband, and consequently drove her away from him.

Then why is Mrs. Erlynne so heroic? The reason is behind the consuming love she shows. She is willing to discard all remote semblances to being a respectable woman in order to save her daughter from making the same tragic mistakes that she made. For the love she bears for her daughter that she forsook twenty years ago, she would even curb her keen and astute intellect. There is something holy about a self-sacrificial love that we can't help but admire. Self-sacrificial love is difficult to make even pretenses at emulating.

In *Woman*, the line dividing the right from the wrong is more clearly defined. Mrs. Arbuthnot is a strictly moral woman, a loving mother careful not to make any shameful wrongs. There is a reason behind her careful attention to morality- when she was young she was tempted into engaging in premarital sex with a young man, later Lord Illingworth, whom she fully expected to marry, but who disappointed her by declining to keep his promise. Thus when she hears that the very same man has offered her son a business proposal, she does not want to let him go, knowing fully well the immorality of the influence the illegitimate father will have on the son's innocence and sweetness.

Such happenings- premarital affairs- were unfortunately quite common even in the Victorian times, and with the passing of time, how people viewed them also changed. In the former half of the era men were excused, owing the misconduct to their carnal appetites. It was something that came, rather apologetically, with being a man. While such an affair would result in the man's taking the blame, they were still tacitly condoned for their misdemeanors. They couldn't help it, after all.

With the latter half of the era, however, the passing time marked a startling change in the perception of the people. Suddenly, the idea that a woman could allow such a thing to happen to her became unimaginably corrupt. Extramarital affairs fell entirely on the woman's shame and blame. The men involved in the affair were no longer only excused- they were forgotten. The entire trend of blaming the woman became a social phenomenon that would continue to influence later social values.

Wilde was very aware of how the people viewed such happenings, and knew that the people's condemnation would fall more on Mrs. Arbuthnot than on Lord Illingworth. Therefore he endowed Illingworth with a perfectly unlikable personality. Illingworth is a fascinating character in all of Wilde's works since he is the sole character that is a dandy, like Wilde himself, yet remains unlikable. Algernon in *The Importance of Being Earnest*, Lord Goring in *An Ideal Husband*, and even Lord Darlington in *Lady Windermere's Fan* are some of the most alluring characters to live in plays. The refinedness with which they speak and the absolute poise with which they behave captivate us with their faintly unearthly beauty.

But not so for Lord Illingworth. When Mrs. Allonby challenges him to describe women as a sex, he immediately responds, "Sphinxes without secrets." Later, when he is talking alone to Mrs. Arbuthnot, he tells her that she was possibly the "nicest plaything" he had. Lord Illingworth's contemptuous treatment of women, and the superciliousness with which he treats them, is a far cry from the Victorian gentleman- he is a "dandy", but he is a crude playboy who has none of the fundamental deference or respect for women. Here is a man who enjoys relationships with women for the sake of the pleasure they derive.

Wilde's searing criticism reaches its peak here. This play is a defense of how even the most perfect dandy, the gentleman of the highest social rank in the Victorian times, can fall lower than the classic "fallen woman" of the era. Lord Illingworth receives the ultimate insult, being slapped with a glove- by his former mistress- because he refuses to acknowledge until the end the human beauty innate in Mrs. Arbuthnot. If only Lord Illingworth had admitted the moral superiority of Mrs. Arbuthnot he would not have fallen quite so low on the social scale. Mrs. Arbuthnot, who has a touching love for her son and a keen sense of morality due to the mistake she had made in her youth, is brought to perfection by acknowledging the flaws of the dandy that does not recognize the innate rights of women. Moral arguments apart, Lord Illingworth ultimately fails because he does not recognize women at their true value, and Mrs. Arbuthnot rises because she does.

Does this show of need for the recognition of women's rights, necessarily show a need in the change of perception for smarter women? I think not. In any of Wilde's plays, the ideal woman seems to be the trivial woman whose life flows on lines following those of Mabel Chiltern's, from *An Ideal Husband*, or perhaps Cecily Cardew's, from *The Importance of Being Earnest*. Indeed, both the woman who are clever in *An Ideal Husband*- Gertrude Chiltern and Laura Cheveley- each represent some type of vice. Gertrude Chiltern illustrates the tendency in women to idolize what they see as worthy of idolization; Laura Cheveley represents the deceitfulness that some women use in order to further their own selfish interests. Smart is never by itself a virtue, and often coupled with others it still remains a vice.

But the very fact that Wilde continuously brings up the issue of women's strengths lends power to the opinion that Wilde was a keen supporter of it. It might be that he did, it might be that he didn't. But the reason that this doubt itself has grounds on which to appear, lies in the fact that Wilde endows his women, along with their weaknesses, with strength. The weaknesses suggest a need for their words and sights to be cultivated; their strengths suggest that their words and rights need to be recognized.

Mrs. Warren's Profession & Pygmalion

Introduction- Mrs. Warren's Profession

I first read *Mrs. Warren's Profession* in the Norton Anthology of English Literature when I was in 9th grade. The Norton Anthology was a big, old-fashioned, dog-eared book with the compact weight and the wafer-thin pages of a dictionary, and with the notes of my aunt's college lectures littering the margins of *Ozymandias* and *The Rime of the Ancient Mariner*. It was always a fun book to have around, a treasure trove for bored moments, an excellent stimulator for sleepy seconds, and I kept it at school as a toy for the inevitable bits and pieces of spare time that were bound to appear no matter how busy I was.

The first play I read in the book was that of another Irish author, Oscar Wilde, whose scintillating wit was admirably displayed in *The Importance of Being Earnest*. Having enjoyed the play so much, I was indignant when I read that contemporary Irish playwright George Bernard Shaw had deemed it to be "essentially hateful" and that "it leaves me with a sense of having wasted my evening." I recall seething, heavens, man, let's see how well you write.

On the next page- like an answer to a challenge- was that very Shaw's play, *Mrs. Warren's Profession*, and I read it avidly. The play was not merely a play; it was in itself an argument that seemed to be condensed into a brick and thrown at the window of society, and now the author was mocking the shattered panes for a response. For a brief moment I joined the embarrassed Victorian audience that would have heard the issues under the words of the play, and then- I swept aside the embarrassment as boldly as Vivie Warren would have, and I gave Shaw this much: maybe, if a man only wrote as heavily as he did, he would have a right to criticize Oscar Wilde's more lighthearted plays.

But then, again, that was before I read-

Introduction- Pygmalion

It's a queer trait with me that whenever I am stressed out I start yowling like a cat.

A lot of people have commented over it, and it's earned me a fair share of nicknames. Dolphin, for one, and Bat, since sometimes my squeaks of distress range high and people think it's something only slightly removed from sonar. And then of course I had Cat and

Panther and Cub. Where "cub" came from, I have no idea. When I asked, the girl who called me that sniffed and said, "Why, a *cub* cub-" so I was left to conclude that even she didn't know.

When I entered high school, I earned my favorite nickname: Eliza Doolittle.

Ms. Lowett was the one who gave me the name. I was, of course, reading *Pygmalion* at the time- we had a Greek mythology revival of sorts in the class, and in the library I happened to notice a book with that word lettered on the spine. Pygmalion- that beautiful tale of the sculptor whose love had moved even the gods. How wonderful.

But when I read it I found out initially to my dismay and ultimately to my delight that the book was nothing about Greek mythology. What a book it was! Though one part of the script puzzled me: "Ah-ah-ah-ow-ow-oo!"

I took it to Ms. Lowett, who was my Composition teacher at the time, and asked her to read it. "It'll be quicker to watch *My Fair Lady*," she smiled as she shook her head. But when I kept on begging her to read it she finally complied and gave me a quick rendition. I was doubled over with laughter.

"It's not very accurate," Ms. Lowett said when she got over her own laughing fit, and she invited me to try. I imitated her to the best of my ability and Ms. Lowett blinked with surprise.

"Why, you're good at it! Do you have any more sounds you can make?"

By the time I ran her through a few more of my SOS calls she was calling me Eliza Doolittle and the name continued for the rest of the year.

The Similarity of Shaw's Femmes Determined

Having grown up in a world where the last vestiges of inequality between the sexes, if there even were any left, were quickly dissolving, and indeed being replaced by an appreciation for the talented, able woman, I find it difficult to believe that until not too long ago women were seen as "the inferior sex." Yet it must have been so, judging by the literature of bygone years. Literature, after all, tends to mirror the mores and trends of its time.

At first the sole function of a woman was to bear children for her husband, and her first duty was to look as ornamental as possible. Then the fixation with ornamentation changed from duty to function, and a woman's duty was establishing social positions within their own unique hierarchy by means of receptions, dinners, at home days, and teas. Social awareness began to grow from the

1800s, pioneered by Olympe de Gouges and Mary Wollstonecraft Shelley; but it was only in the twentieth century that women began battling for rights in earnest.

Late in the nineteenth century, then, when Irish playwright George Bernard Shaw wrote plays starring pragmatic female characters with a blunt desire for either social or material wealth, the characters themselves were unique since they were largely unprecedented in literature; but given the slow social changes already reverberating throughout the society the plays had ample grounds on which they could be favorably received, especially among new-thinking women. As Shaw himself said, "It is a play for women··· it was written for women··· it has been performed and produced mainly through the determination of women that it should be performed and produced." Compared to his contemporary Irish playwright Oscar Wilde, whose female characters still largely retained their passive, calm, lethargic Victorian etiquette (with the rare exception of Mrs. Cheveley in *An Ideal Husband*), Shaw's characters are refreshingly honest and straightforward. Even in plays that seem widely disparate, there remains a very tangible similarity between the main characters.

Of all of Shaw's plays possibly the best-known one is *Pygmalion*, which also takes credit as one of the most misunderstood plays. Starting from its very first production to the musical adaptation of *My Fair Lady* many years later, *Pygmalion* has been interpreted as a story of a poor girl rising in social status to become a lady and potentially the lover of her teacher, a gentleman. Although Shaw was enraged at his play being thus understood, neither the later productions nor the movies obeyed Shaw's wishes.

Another one of Shaw's plays received almost the exact opposite reaction to what *Pygmalion* had received, condemned in its first reviews for the brutal candidness with which it dealt on the subjects of prostitution and incest. *Mrs. Warren's Profession* relates the story of a girl who is pragmatic, businesslike, and utterly unromantic. When the girl finds out the source of the wealth that has enabled her mother to put her through an expensive education and make plans for her as a lady, she decides to sever all relationships with her mother and earn money for herself.

At a brief glance, no two plays could be more different than *Pygmalion* and *Mrs. Warren's Profession*. However, upon closer inspection, the readers find a startling symmetry between the two plays, especially in the similarities between the characters of Eliza Doolittle and Vivie Warren. Strong, pragmatic, and realistic, both characters are variations of Shaw's archetypal females- the new-thinking, working woman.

Let us first inspect *Pygmalion*, starring Eliza Doolittle. Eliza Doolittle is a girl of "perhaps eighteen, perhaps twenty, hardly older." (Shaw, 11) In the beginning she starts out as "not at all a romantic figure" (Shaw, 10) although "her features are no worse than theirs [the ladies']." (Shaw, 11) As time progresses, however, Eliza slowly grows more attractive; after a few months of training by Professor Higgins and Colonel Pickering she "produces an impression of such remarkable distinction and beauty" (Shaw, 59) that the ladies who meet her are all quite flustered. At the end of the promised six months of training, the strength of her presence at the ball of her test is so strong that "some of the younger ones at the back stand on their chairs to see." (Shaw, 71)

Eliza, however, is not only a malleable student. Her clean-cut moral standards show in her response to Professor Higgins's suggestion that she marry, when she doesn't know what to do with herself anymore, having been so fantastically declassed. She sharply replies, "We were above that at the corner of Tottenham Court Road··· I sold flowers, I didn't sell myself." (Shaw, 78) Eliza is also strong-willed without being arrogant[3]. When Higgins ignores her plea for a little kindness, Eliza snaps after enduring months of bullying at his hands. She fights back, coming to the state where she "snaps his head off on the faintest provocation, or on none··· she stands up to him so ruthlessly that the Colonel has to ask her from time to time to be kinder to Higgins". (Shaw, 119)

---

3) Two of the most admirable qualities that can be found in a woman. I loved Eliza for her unconventional acts. Eliza would have been considered unwomanly by the standards of the time, but for me, her sweet sassiness and independence was more than enough to make me love her. I believe the same would apply for many readers.

At first glance Vivie Warren is very different from the beggar-turned-princess Eliza Doolittle. Aged 22, Vivie is "an attractive specimen of the sensible, able, highly-educated young middle-class Englishwoman… prompt, strong, confident, self-possessed." (Shaw, 14) Thoroughly unromantic and with a strong aversion to anything that takes time without being profitable, arts included, her only interests lie in making money from doing work. Her dreams are to "work at actuarial calculations and conveyancing… with one eye on the Stock Exchange all the time." (Shaw, 17) A graduate of the University of Cambridge with high honors in mathematics, she feels no need for further education, and neither does she dream of rising in social circles.

Vivie, too, is not without her problems. When she first finds that her mother derived her wealth through the management of brothels, rising from the worst of poverty to a comfortable state, Vivie calls her "a wonderful woman… stronger than all of England." (Shaw, 38) Vivie does not necessarily approve of the venture itself, but she does approve that her mother worked in an efficient way to gain profits. Later, however, she learns that her mother is still gaining profits from the brothels, and she becomes disgusted with her mother. Vivie tells her, "I don't want to be worthless… I am like you: I must have work, and must make more money than I spend. But my work is not yours, and my way is not your way." (Shaw, 60)

So now we see that the two girls are both feisty, independent, attractive to a certain degree, and with strict standards of morality in their respective ways, but those are traits that any heroine might share. What makes these two uniquely similar? Firstly, both are willing to undergo a good deal to accomplish their goals. Eliza spends six months of being completely dominated and bullied by Professor Higgins in order to learn to become like a lady, and Vivie sends back money checks from her mother once she learns where that money is coming from. Secondly, both girls are relatively free from romantic interests, and do not let their lack get in the way of their career. The movies and productions that portray Eliza and Professor Higgins as a couple are disapproved even now by Shaw's ghost. Eliza might be "superstitiously devoted to them both [Colonel Pickering and Professor Higgins], more entirely and frankly after her marriage than before it" (Shaw, 113), as the sequel suggests, but her husband is still Freddie. Vivie also engages in a briefly romantic tangle with Frank Gardner, but after hearing her mother's profession she decides that love and beauty are not for her, and repulses Frank's approaches firmly, as she "tears the note up and tosses the pieces into the wastepaper basket without a second thought" (Shaw, 61) in the last act. It is also interesting to note that even the names of the girls' love interests are similar- Freddy and Frank.

Thirdly, both girls suffer heavily from their parents. For one, Eliza's father is a common dustman who does not care too much for his daughter. He offers to sell his daughter for fifty pounds to Professor Higgins when he first hears of Eliza's moving there, and his present mistress is his sixth wife. Vivie's mother is even worse- she arranges and manages a string of "hotels" that provide cheap comfort for men and a dependable, substantial profit for herself. Throughout the entire play, it remains a point of mystery who Vivie's father is, and while there is reason to believe it might be either Croft or Gardner Sr. judging by Shaw's various manuscripts, Mrs. Warren herself keeps the silence, implying the possible presence of even a third man. Thus it can be seen that Vivie's mother has as little qualms with these extramarital affairs as the girls at the brothels that she manages.

As Shaw describes parents of both heroines- respectively, Eliza's father and Vivie's mother- it is interesting to see that while he limns them with pity and pathos in his eye, he never describes them outright negatively. Alfred Doolittle is a bumbling character filled with the sense of his own importance. In his roughneck speeches there is a tang of the very honest as only the low classes can be. All in all, with the progression of the play, the reader comes to love Alfred Doolittle and his preposterous but true philosophy. Mrs. Warren is harder to love, especially as she is somewhat vulgar and often given to histrionics when she feels like her daughter is slipping away from her. But it never reaches the point of repellence; and from the viewpoint of a sympathetic audience her dramatics simply elucidates on the pathos of the character. After all, Shaw is not aiming to destroy the literary engagingness of the characters; he is aiming to address the society and its problems so that due measures can be taken to solve the issues.

Given the similarity of Vivie and Lizzie, it is interesting to pursue further points of symmetry between the two plays that come about due to the characteristics of the "new-thinking woman": the relation between the creator and the created, and the irony in both titles. Firstly, both girls repulse a continuing influence of their "creator"- for Eliza, Professor Higgins, who has trained not only her accent but also her social ability to act like a lady; for Vivie, her mother, who has paid for her education until her college years. Both of them are independent and wish to be seen as equals with their creators, and both of them show it: in *Pygmalion*, Eliza says, "I know I'm a common ignorant girl, and you a book-learned gentleman; but I'm not dirt under your feet." In the beginning of *Mrs. Warren's Profession*, Praed warns Mrs. Warren to treat Vivie like an adult, to which Mrs. Warren laughs, "Young people have to get all that nonsense taken out of them, and a good deal more besides." (Shaw, 20) Later, however, when Vivie is saying goodbye to her, she asks kindly, "Won't you shake hands?" (Shaw, 61) implying that the two are on equal footing. The reason both of them part with their creators is because they treat them like inferiors, ignoramuses that must either be bullied in Eliza's case, or hoodwinked and led into higher society in Vivie's case. The new-thinking woman abhors having decisions made for her; she must make them herself.

It is natural, therefore, that the titles for both plays should be ironic; in a world where young ladies have so far only been petted and praised in generally non-individualistic ways, these plays are two bricks of social messages crying out for the further development of woman individuality. *Pygmalion* is ironic since the crux of the play lies not in the creator's role of creating; it lies in why Pygmalion and Galatea can never be lovers- "Galatea never does quite like Pygmalion: his relation to her is too godlike to be altogether agreeable." (Shaw, 119) Given the hierarchal nature of their relationship, a mutually satisfying love is impossible. Likewise, *Mrs. Warren's Profession* is ironic, firstly because the one thing that cannot be mentioned anywhere in society for what it is- the management of brothels- has become the play's title, but secondly because this is, again, what has driven Vivie away from her mother. Mrs. Warren's job is to hoodwink young girls and pull them into prostitution. Similarly, she also tries to hoodwink Vivie, stopping her from thinking about the source of the money but instead where she could use it. Vivie loathes this deception; she does not want to be placed at the mercies of the deceptions of another woman.

Today the only type of woman we have is the "new-thinking woman" of the past, and the idea of another type of woman seems so alien to us as to be laughable. Vivie and Eliza are both characters we admire and communicate with, since they are not afraid to speak their minds when the need arises, since they think for themselves, and since they are strong and pragmatic and realistic. Bernard Shaw's admirably written plays, the symmetry between the two plays and the techniques that showcase the individualities of Vivie and Eliza, serve as a testimony that once these characters were the revolutionary cutting-edge characters of their day, but even in widely different circumstances from ours, these women were admirable. For the people who think for themselves, making their decisions and molding their own lives- whatever the scenario- are always admirable.

A Doll's House

Introduction

There was one literary term I never really liked hearing: Ibsenism.

I don't really know why I didn't like it so much, especially when I knew so little about it. Henrik Ibsen, for all I knew, was a Norwegian playwright. When I Googled him I found a man looking faintly like a sterner version of Father Christmas, with solemn eyes peering out from behind his very round spectacles. The father of realism, the man who had most heavily influenced Oscar Wilde and Bernard Shaw, my two favorite playwrights: Henrik Johan Ibsen.

Mr. Parry found out about this not too long after he had cured me of my initial aversion to Black literature (see *Their Eyes Were Watching God*) and he slapped his knees and fairly howled with laughter. When he had wiped the last of the mirth out of his eyes, he leaned forward, still chuckling, and met my shamefaced gaze evenly though good-humoredly.

"I swear, you feisty little kitten, you'll be the death of me one day. What am I to do with you?"

"Do with what?" I asked meekly.

"Why, your dislikes. Especially when I can guess what you'll be thinking after you read what I'll give you."

I pouted slightly and Mr. Parry laughed.

"Take your medicine bravely, my dear. Don't worry, it's like cough syrup, you'll enjoy it."

"Will it make me fall asleep?"

Lightly slapping my hand for my pert question, Mr. Parry wheeled around and flicked on the computer deftly. Soon the printer was shuddering out sheaves of warm, printed paper.

Mr. Parry stood up and gave a mock frown, though his smile somewhat ruined the effect.

"Let me remind you once more, if anyone asks where you had the play printed, where do you say?"

"Downstairs in the first floor lobby."

My obedient lie made Mr. Parry's smile grow wider.

"Good. I hope you know how much Mr. Lee yelled at me last time for letting you print up here."

"Oh, well. I'm sure you didn't cry."

"I'm sure I did. Tell me what you think of it, now, after you finish reading it. If you still don't like Ibsenism, I'm a frog."

I sighed in half defeat.

"You'll never be a frog, Mr. Parry. Never."

Madame Nora's Identity

Before I read it, I was always curious why *A Doll's House* was named the way it was. As I said, I really wasn't interested in Ibsenism; I liked Oscar Wilde's plays and I liked George Bernard Shaw's plays, but the reason I liked both, respectively, were completely different, and I couldn't imagine that the same influence could have acted on both of them.

Besides, we were studying modernist Korean literature in our language classes just then, and the modernist novella we had to read for homework alluded once to *A Doll's House*, which probably influenced my conception somewhat. What happened was, the woman who had been inspired by the play in her college years was now a miserly debt collector who would mercilessly rake the last coins from a starving family to add to her own fortune. She had also formerly been- horror of horrors!- the mistress of a Japanese official when the Japanese were in control over Korea. I now know that issues of patriotism and generosity have nothing to do with Ibsenism or *A Doll's House*, and I suppose the author had used the play as a symbol to draw exactly how far the woman had fallen- and how forward-thinking and commendable Henrik Ibsen's play was- but the fact that such a decadent character could have once appreciated the play somehow degraded it in my value.

As always this childish prejudice got me in trouble; or rather, it got me caught, since Mr. Parry was like a bloodhound whenever he glimpsed even a tiny bit of aversion on my part against any genre of literature. Once again I was given extra reading homework. I will frankly say that the first play I read, *Romersholm*, is today one of my least-liked Ibsen plays, but it did intrigue me enough to initiate a quest in search of more enjoyable ones. In quick succession I hunted up and read *Ghosts* and *When We Dead Awaken*, and reminded of the allusion that had led me to my initial distaste of Ibsenism, I devoured *A Doll's House* as well.

Curiously, and ironically, the play that led me to open my arms to Ibsenism was *A Doll's House*. Mr. Parry enjoyed the irony almost as much as I did and didn't leave off teasing me for a month. I suppose, though, it was because I had expected so little from the play, but had in fact gained so much from it, that I was all the more enchanted by it. If being intoxicated meant anything, it must have been something close to what I felt: that heady feeling of liberty so strong it was a burden to take it on. -Why! That a woman could be so free as to speak her mind thus, disregarding all senses of propriety, social morality, and duty! For Nora, when she willingly stepped out of Torvald's sphere of life, took her life from Torvald's strong, capable, yet insensible hands, and placed it in her own. With that motion she also shifted the burden of the consequences of her actions on to her own shoulders.

To properly appreciate Nora's bravery it will be necessary to inspect the circumstances preceding her decision. Nora, when we first see her, is only juvenile; her immature way of thinking, judging, and lying is all too evident from the beginning. Her faults show not only through the way she comports herself, but also through the way she and her husband interact. Firstly, Nora, disregarding the fact that the family is not very comfortable economically, spends a good deal of money on her Christmas shopping- she has a child's sense of finance; or rather, lack of it. Secondly, although Torvald has directly forbidden her to do so, Nora indulges her sweet tooth in macaroons and shamelessly lies to her husband that she "should not think of going against your [Torvald's] wishes." (Ibsen, 5) Although these lies and immaturities have the effect of drawing Nora as an adorable child that must be taken care of, and endears Nora so completely to the audience from the beginning that disliking her in the middle of the play would be difficult, lies are still lies, and incapability still incapability. The minor lie, in special, may not seem very important, but the continuity of these small deceptions between the couple signifies that the couple's relationship cannot quite be as smooth as it initially seems.

Nora's sweetly childlike guile and lack of sense leads her husband to tease her "my little lark," "my little squirrel," and even "my little spendthrift." It is obvious that the relationship is not a healthy one between husband and wife, but rather more of a stilted one between the superior one teaching and the inferior one learning, the superior one as adult and the inferior one as child. This would not be half so problematic if the intellectual gap between the two were actually so wide, but that is not the case. Nora, though she does seem to retain the childlike quality of having no division between right and wrong throughout the play, is not quite as thoughtless as she seems. Although it is not proper for a woman to hold business transactions with a man in the mores of the era, and indeed is never proper for a woman to hold monetary transactions without informing her husband of the incident, Nora has borrowed money under forged bonds and is paying back by doing typing-work. Completely disregarding the immorality of forgery, Nora boasts of her accomplishments to her disapproving friend, saying "Oh, if it is a wife who has any head for business- a wife who has the wit to be a little bit clever-" (Ibsen, 11)

By the middle of the play, then, it is evident that Nora is a great deal shrewder than she seems; she has a clear business head which she uses admirably, though not always morally. Indeed, she has a child's sense of morals: the good intentions justify the bad means in any cases, and harm done to any of the characters carried along in her deception is utterly disregarded. Yet, as in a child, her sense of thoughtless morals and her loyalty to her husband is wonderful and adorable, and there is an additional pluckiness about her that makes it impossible for the reader to want to chastise her, unless it is for her occasional thoughtlessness.

Problems arise in earnest, however, when Nora's dishonesty is in danger of being revealed to the world. Completely changing his demeanor from that of the tender, wise husband, Torvald scornfully refuses to listen to what Nora has to say in defense- "Oh, don't let us have any silly excuses." (Ibsen, 56) He mourns the disgrace his wife's dishonesty will cause him, and he focuses his attentions not on their relationship but on saving public appearances, telling Nora, "From this moment happiness is not the question; all that concerns us is to save the remains, the fragments, the appearance-" (Ibsen, 57) Nora, initially shocked by but increasingly comprehending of the situation, and finally seeing their relationship in a clear light for the first time, grows cold towards Torvald.

When Torvald receives news almost immediately afterwards that the disgraceful secret will be in no way be divulged, he immediately reverts to his original attitude, petting Nora again: "Try and calm yourself, and make your mind easy again, my frightened little singing-bird." (Ibsen, 58) His old consciousness of the husband being entirely in control over his wife reveals itself in the next phrase: "There is something so indescribably sweet and satisfying, to a man, in the knowledge that he has forgiven his wife… it seems as if… he has given her a new life." (Ibsen, 58) It is evident that the stilted relationship between the two people will not change- the husband will always remain the teaching, indulgent parent; the wife will remain the learning, dependent child. The play ends with Nora walking out on Torvald, saying that this relationship cannot exist any longer. In response to Torvald's statement, "Before all else, you are a wife and a mother," Nora retorts, "I believe that before all else I am a reasonable human being… or, at all events, that I must try and become one." (Ibsen, 61)

This tragic event is what ironically brings the real Nora, the best part of Nora, forth. In finding that her husband is not someone who is similar enough to her ideals for the two to be able to make a happy couple, Nora becomes detached, quiet, cold, and analytical. Having been pushed beyond her immaturity to have to find a point of maturity allows Nora to see the situation clearly and take matters into her own hands. In the space of hours, Nora has turned from a childish girl who needs to be guided in her everyday life, into a wise woman who prioritizes not by sentiment but by logic. What she believes to be most important is finding her identity, who she truly is; not acting as a doll-wife to her husband or a doll-mother to her children; and it is according to this ideal which she recognizes as necessary to fulfill that she is able to decide to leave her husband and her home.

It must be said that while everything is admirable about this play, the change that Nora shows in her growth from child to woman is too sudden to be realistic. In the beginning of the play Ibsen utilizes to his maximum ability the social preconception of the ideal wife: a sweet little thing flying about to carry out everything related to home, but necessarily under the complete rule of her husband, and continuously needing his guidance to stay on a completely morally right path. Nora might have intellectual benefits above that of a child's, but it must be admitted, what makes Nora so charming is because she is just a child in an adult's guise. Otherwise it would be difficult to forgive her.

Her childishness continues to manifest itself evenly throughout the play. When she is waiting for Torvald's fury to burst, not knowing when it is that Torvald will find out about her deception, she acts in a supremely childish way: she stops him from discovering the deception by playing the first bars of the Tarantella, which she must dance, and pretending that she has forgotten everything that Torvald taught her- a child's play, if anything. And almost like a form of a child's desperate tantrum, she dances, as Torvald notes, "as if your life depended on it." (Ibsen, 44) At the very moment when she has decided to leave the house she talks to herself in hoarse whispers like children do when they are making a scary decision. But suddenly, at the first hint of Torvald's rage, she "looks steadily at him··· with a growing look of coldness in her face" (Ibsen, 56) and from then on speaks in a tone that we did not expect from Nora the adorable. She has become a woman in the space of a few minutes. The metamorphosis is as startling and as disturbing as a slap on the face.

But this startling change is necessary, since if it does not contribute to the credibility of the play, it plays a certain role symbolically. The moment Nora feels herself to be under no obligation to Torvald, she allows herself to grow into a true woman. She is no longer tied to her husband and thus is no longer obliged to act like a child to him. She will treat him, like a grown human being to another grown human being, indulging in a part of her that neither husband nor wife allowed to be manifested so far.

Often it is difficult to follow what one believes to be true or important due to the limiting social factors. Yet Nora, knowing what was truly important, ignored all the possible social consequences and instead turned to the more important, fundamental issue of finding herself. Nora stands as a symbol for all of those who stay true to themselves and learn to break free of societal standards.

Thus *A Doll's House* is a truly powerful play about the importance of women- and indeed, humanity in general- determining and finding what is truly important.

Hedda Gabler

Introduction

My sister never likes reading sad books. She is a very loyal person and a sympathetic reader. Once she swears her allegiances at the beginning of the book, there is no turning her back; she does not swerve, and neither can she bear to stand and watch. There are so many beautiful stories that I have read and then recommended to my sister, but she has refused to take my word for it. She knew they would leave her in a somewhat worse mood than she had formerly been, and therefore, she would not budge.

But then that is my sister, who is worlds apart from me in the issue of reading. I am cold, I am economical with my affections; I pride myself on being a taciturn reader, not apt to give myself up to emotions due to the book. I rarely associate with the characters in the books, preferring to watch their progress impersonally from the sidelines.

It came as a surprise to me, therefore, when the capricious and dominating Hedda Gabler came across as strangely attractive. Something about her personality, full of conflicting emotions and

desires and unrealistic ideals, clicked with something within me-
the villain that all of us secretly long to be once in a while. Hedda
personified and fulfilled that role. She became a part of me, thus
dragging me headlong into her desires, her confidence, her life; in
short, the plot.

My favorite Ibsen play still remains, as I mentioned, *A Doll's
House*. As much of a miniature spitfire as Nora may be, she is not
the incomprehensible queenly creature that Hedda is. It is safer to
love Nora than Hedda.

But Hedda must be respected and revered and, since her
inscrutable haughtiness in dealing with life will not allow her to
suffer such a degradation as to be dissected, she must be vivisected.
Throughout the surgery the question remains: how does Ibsen
endow Hedda with the captivating power she has?

How the Father of Realism Defied Reality

After I first met Hedda Gabler I spent some time wondering if
she would universally be acknowledged as a captivating character.
There were so many reasons not to like her- she was calculating,
insulting, unsympathetic, and imperious; her cynical moods were as
dark and clouded as a noir picture developed under light exposure.

But knowing her faults did nothing to change my own attraction.

We had just finished covering *The Catcher in the Rye* in literature class, and most of my friends were either captivated or sickened by Holden's childish cynicism to the degree that they had started to disregard all other cynical characters. So no help was to be found there. Not many people would have talked about Hedda with me anyways. Modernist plays were not a universally liked genre in my school- as in any school- and more often than not, reading them earns you the reputation of "nerd." I had already been so universally classified as a literature freak that one more queer literary taste couldn't possibly further ruin my reputation. I had none to salvage in regard to literature. The teachers who I turned to for help, only smiled Cheshire-cat wise smiles and refused to tell me until I had made my own judgments.

I couldn't, for a long time, so I let it be and spent my time investigating other books, less damaging to my reputation and more catholically enjoyed. Only recently did I remember to return to poor Hedda, whom I had halfheartedly accused and denounced, but whose fate I had forgotten to finalize. It was time to announce the sentence and bang the gavel, make up my mind on a character who I had neglected for far too long.

But before the gavel could be banged, there were pieces of evidence to reinvestigate: Hedda's character to be re-examined, her speeches and her interactions with others to be scrutinized, and the reason of her charm inspected and analyzed to within an inch of her life.

This is where the verdict begins.

The first piece of evidence: Hedda's character. Hedda is many things- capricious, willful, dominating, repellent, attractive- but most of all, she is manipulative. This, her manipulative character, is what makes her so hard to decide whether she is truly captivating or only quasi-captivating. A manipulative person is wonderful when the victim is unaware that he is being manipulated, but once the realization of manipulation strikes, the wonder dies. The person becomes untrustworthy and dangerous. After all, she has tried to gain control. As wonderfully individual and woefully headstrong as humans have been created, lust for control is never excusable in anyone else but ourselves. At the same time there cannot help but be a secret grudging sympathy in every heart, since this lust for power is present in every individual and headstrong personality.

In the beginning we do not see much of Hedda's manipulative character; we only see a woman already weary of her marriage by the end of the honeymoon. Hedda is tired. Since her immediate desire of having a famous, prestigious husband is nearly secure, she makes minimal efforts to rise to even lethargic heights, and the discontent arising from her life now that the initial clamor is over, has such a strong, immediate presence as to be tangible. She wonders, somewhat idly, if she could possibly bear her life to continue in such a fashion. Such an unflattering view of her leads the reader to wonder if she was always such a despondent character, and if her beauty was the only thing that made her such a strong presence as to earn her the reverence of her husband's family.

Her discontent is not yet climactic. It is only when rivals enter the scene that her aversion of the status quo stimulates her back into action. Immediately she grows back into the powerful character that she must have been before we first saw her. Her silver tongue works smoothly on her adversaries, petting them and beguiling them, convincing them that she is their best friend and sworn supporter, all the while during which she plots and plans so that they will move accordingly to her will, like dumb wooden chess pieces slid into formation by her slim white hand. The number of people she contrives into moving as she desires, and the degree to which they change to fit the mold, are remarkable: her husband, her childhood schoolmate, her former lover all undergo significant metamorphoses under Hedda's very capable hands. Her husband becomes morally stricken, her childhood schoolmate distraught with agony but granted new hope, and her former lover driven with despair to the point of suicide.

With the facts laid bare in front of us, Hedda can be nothing more than a cold-blooded maniac. We say that she is understandable, if nothing else, since her desire for control is one shared by humanity in general. But what is it that makes her so charming? What gives her that strange attractive force that no one else in her shoes would be able to command? The secret lies in the type of world she seeks to create. Hedda is, in a way, the mini-god of her sphere, and she seeks ways to fill her world with what is beautiful and ideal. To accomplish this Hedda must remove all other factors that might cast the slightest shadow on what she seeks to create- meaning that she must be queen of her world, and all the males in her world must be subservient to her. The very fact that the name of the play is named *Hedda Gabler,* not Hedda Tesman, shows how she chooses to identify herself: not as the wife of George Tesman, but as the daughter of General Gabler, whose pistols she uses to reaffirm, crucially, that she is the one who controls all of her life and the lives of others. As doubtable as the morality of her actions sometimes can be, her longings for a world of ideal and beauty that she can control is pathetic and pitiable, and thus the consistent loyalty she shows towards the ideals she holds is admirable.

Admittedly, the line until which she can be understood has its limits. There is no one who will not be able to understand Hedda's burning the manuscript of a book that might potentially cast her husband into a nameless oblivion forever- if only Hedda had done it for such reasonable purposes. But it is for a more sinister reason, and yet simultaneously due to a more humane emotion, that Hedda chooses to burn the manuscript: out of spite for her own failed life. Again, the reader is stuck in the heart-wrenching crossfire between sympathy and understanding, admire, and brutal judgment.

Hedda's mercurial character, then, gains some justification, but the full changeability of her character would not be as clear had Ibsen not symbolized it through the form of address within the play- the second piece of evidence. Crucial to the play is how the characters call and refer to one another. For the most part how the characters call each other "you"- *du* for endearment and *de* for formality- heavily influences the play and how the relationships between two people are defined. Hedda flatly refuses to call her aunt-in-law *du*, reasserting herself as being independent from the consequences of her marriage. A while later, however, she calls an old schoolmate who was not on very amicable terms with herself in the years past, as *du*, guiling her into a seemingly innocent relationship.

Why is this mode of address so important? It again shows how crucial control is to Hedda. With the people she know she can easily control, calling each other *du* is inconsequential. As much of a symbol of love as it is, love also carries with it the implicit concept of control over each other. As long as the loved subject is entirely within her manipulation, Hedda is open to the term. Indeed, it is the characters who cannot be so easily maintained that Hedda is reticent to address as *du*. These include Hedda's old lover, who has found new love and inspiration in Hedda's old schoolmate, and Hedda's aunt-in-law, a lady quite self-sacrificial in her love for her nephew.

Hedda is also unwilling to address many other people in anything but formal ways. Hedda only refers to her late father's pistols as "General Gabler's pistols," and the word "father" never escapes her mouth. When she is talking to her former lovers, they are all polite and proper; even when she is talking to her husband, she calls him by his last name rather than his first. Whoever might cause the least amount of danger to Hedda's reign, Hedda repulses. She must be the ruling queen of whatever to come.

Since it is one of those many things that have to be said, and since no one- well, no one in my immediate vicinity, anyways- is there to say it but me, I suppose I will.

The source of Hedda Gabler's charm lies entirely in her fictitiousness. She is a creature that can never exist. Simply like my own Madame Hyde can never exist. She was fleshed in Hedda Gabler before I even knew she existed.

The reason that Hedda is so lovable as an unreal character is that there is no way that a real, living creature, fearing death and loving life, would act as determinedly as she does. Hedda is so completely fixated on beauty and power that she exalts it above the importance of life. The illusion of beauty, and the belief that she has enough power to make whatever that she controls beautiful, spurs her to goad her former lover to his death and finally to kill herself.

In actual human life, there is never a human will so strong that life becomes of secondary consequence. Not so for Hedda. Hedda's life must necessarily be, until the end, controlled by her own will, and completed to the last degree of beauty and ideal. The reader falls in love with Hedda for no other great reason than for this: an admirable consistency in her thoughts and actions, until the moment she dies.

So now it is evident why Hedda Gabler is such a wonderful character. By the very definition of her character it is impossible to make her realistic, since the ways she works is completely fictional. This also ensures that she can stay true to her character without flouting the laws of comprehension. Ibsen, the father of realism, by posing Hedda as the star of his most famous play, might have set himself up for criticisms by critics who refuse to relinquish their corrupted ideal. But he made Hedda Gabler unforgettable and special.

A Streetcar Named Desire

Introduction

Junho and I stand in front of the large double-door cupboard, peering at the books through the glass panels. It has almost become a game between us- seeing how slowly we can mop the thin strip of marble that winds between the teachers' desks and the bookshelves, seeing how long we can loiter in front of the shelves without getting yelled at.

A loud stern cough sounds from behind us, and Junho's curls bounce up and down as he resumes mopping, but he looks up to throw me a question.

"What do you want to read?"

I smile. Every time we stand here we ask each other the same question, but we make it a rule, every time, to answer differently. I answer with a question of my own.

"Have you read *Gone With the Wind*?"

"Vivien Leigh for Scarlett O'Hara and Clark Gable for Rhett Butler. Won Best Picture, Best Actress, Best Supporting Actress, Best Director and four other Bests in the 1940 Academy Awards. Really, that lovesick ol' classic?"

Shaking my head at Junho's astounding capacity for memorizing movie-related paraphernalia, I start wiping the high ledges that divide the teachers' desks.

"It's still good. But no, that's not what I want to read."

Junho straightens his back.

"Well, then, what?"

"This one."

Junho's gaze follows my finger to a thin book wedged between *The Complete Collection of Robert Browning's Poems* and *War and Peace*. The legend is small but brave, standing out boldly from the slender little frame.

"Marlon Brando for Stanley Kowalski and Vivien Leigh for Blanche duBois. Vivian Leigh, Kim Hunter, and Karl Malden all won Oscars for that one."

"Do you ever read, Junho? Not watch but read?"

Junho pops open the cupboard door, slips out the slender volume, and places it in my hand.

"Well, now- you can read it for me, can't you?"

"That which we call Blanche by any other name would hardly be as white"

: The Importance of Naming in Streetcar

A Streetcar Named Desire is one of the greatest classical American plays. From Blanche's very first words to Stanley's heartrending cry, "Stella!" the superb alignment of emotions and script makes it unforgettable. The more the script is read, however, it becomes more and more obvious that the play has many levels on which it can be interpreted. Tennessee Williams's genius for naming people and places, and his allusions to specific objects, plays a very significant role in *A Streetcar Named Desire*, exaggerating personalities and highlighting ironies.

Blanche duBois, the protagonist of the play, has by far the most interesting name. When the reader first meets her, "she is daintily dressed in a white suit with a fluffy bodice, necklace and earrings of pearl, white gloves and hat···" (Williams, 5) Later she introduces herself to Mitch saying, "It [duBois] means woods and Blanche means white, so the two together mean white woods." (Williams, 59) Blanche, however, is hardly as white as her name: after losing her husband, then her home, she takes shelter in a shady hotel where her indiscrete sexual misconducts lead her to be kicked out and turned into a social outcast. Her final affair with a seventeen-year-old schoolboy causes the end of her career as a schoolteacher. Her private life, if anything, is black with sin and adultery.

Blanche is not entirely to blame for her deterioration, however. Her first discovery of love with poet Allan Grey is beautiful, like suddenly turning "a blinding light on something that had always been half in shadow." (Williams, 114) When she finds out about Allan's homosexuality, however, she repulses him, leading him to commit suicide, and "the searchlight which had been turned on the world was turned off again and never for one moment since has there been any light that's stronger than this- kitchen- candle…" (Williams, 115) Light, which Blanche shrinks from in real life for fear it will show her age and her diminished beauty, serves to highlight the tragedy and symbolism in Blanche's name. When her world was lit by bright light, Blanche herself was as beautiful and pure as her name; now, older and blackened with sorrow and sin, she cannot bear to see herself in light, since she can no longer find a love as illuminating and true as her first. It is also interesting to note that Allan means "fair, handsome," which can take on two interpretations: firstly, in a literal sense, Allan himself is young and good-looking; secondly, in a more ironic way, the fair and handsome young Allan is a degenerate, a homosexual, whose name is as much of a misnomer as Blanche's.

Stella duBois, Blanche's sister, stands as a foil for Blanche, both in character and in name. "Stella for Star!" (Williams, 10) as Blanche calls her, responds very differently when given the same circumstances. When Stanley grows hot-tempered and abusive at the end of the poker party in Scene 3, Blanche is contemptuous and scorns his ill-breeding, but Stella comes down after a while to enjoy the night with him. It is only at the end, when Blanche's last shreds of lies and self-respect have been completely destroyed, that Stanley manages to have his way with her.

If Stanley Kowalski is the symbol of male sexuality, and thus a stand-in for night, then Stella is the star that shines softly and gently in the night sky, while Blanche is the white that spurns the dark of the night, unable to coexist with it. This is ironic since Blanche has never been "white" and pure since the beginning of the play- her history marks a past as dark and sin-cluttered as night itself. Her hypocrisy, in pretending to act so pure and white, is revealed in Stanley's words as he states his intention to rape her: "We've had this date with each other from the beginning!" (Williams, 162)

Mitchell Howard is another interesting misnomer whose name adds further irony to the play. His touching devotion to his ailing mother, as well as his scrupulous attentions to Blanche in the beginning of the play, makes the meaning of his name, "gift from God," a perfect fit. To Blanche, however, Mitch's betrayal is the most painful one in the book. Since she had hopes of settling down there and marrying Mitch, the closest the neighborhood had to a

"Southern gentleman," his disgust with her and his attempt to rape her completely destroys her. The audience gets a glimpse of Blanche "drinking fairly steadily since Mitch left" (Williams, 104), with no attempts on her side to even hide her total deterioration. Blanche is out of the reaches of God's gift.

The names of places are also important in *Streetcar*. Most iconic is the address of the Kowalski's: "They told me to take a streetcar named Desire, and then transfer to one called Cemeteries and ride six blocks and get off at- Elysian Fields!" (Williams, 6) The streetcar named Desire, after which the play is named, is a car that both Stella and Blanche have boarded. Stella, however, has willingly boarded it, and made it a part of her address, whereas Blanche says "It brought me here. -Where I'm not wanted and where I'm ashamed to be⋯" (Williams, 81) Here, she is not referring only to her current circumstance- she is referring to the entire train of events that has dragged her down from her initial pure state to her present sinful state. This connects again to their names: Stella the Star openly embraces the night and its lust; Blanche refuses to admit that she is anything less than white, and cannot bear to associate with it.

The middle step, Cemeteries, is symbolic as well. Every time Blanche carried out her sexual desires with men, she was first shunned then thrown out by the society, thus dying a symbolic death in each area. "Cemeteries" is a car she knows doubly well, however, because this vicious cycle also played a crucial role in the loss of her home, Belle Reve. "Our improvident grandfathers and father and uncles and brothers exchanged the land for their epic fornications··· finally all that was left··· was··· about twenty acres of ground, including a graveyard, to which now all··· have retreated." (Williams, 44) Blanche herself has witnessed five deaths, four of those her direct family numbers and one her young husband, and the last "block" the car Cemeteries has to go before it reaches Elysian Fields is her own death- her mental destruction.

Elysian Fields, also Elysium, stands clearly in contrast with Belle Reve, French for "beautiful dream." With the burdens of her family's death weighing heavily on her expenses, Blanche had no choice but to give up her home. She receives papers for them, all of which she gives to Stanley, ironically remarking "I think it's wonderfully fitting that Belle Reve should finally be this bunch of old papers in your big, capable hands!" (Williams, 44) The irony lies in the fact that Stanley enjoys women as much as the former grandfathers and fathers that sold away the land. But having given up the last traces of her "beautiful dream" to the person she trusts least, the best and only place left for Blanche is Elysium- the heaven of Greek mythology, but a place where she comes to finally be destructed.

Two other places of importance in the play are the city Laurel, where Blanche stayed before she came to the Kowalski's, and the hotel Flamingo. Both places smack strongly of irony. Traditionally, laurels stand as a symbol of victory and champions; yet Laurel is the city where Blanche begins losing her battle against herself in earnest, losing self-control and abstinence. Flamingos, too, are symbols of elegance, grace, and wealth, the opposite of the lifestyle Blanche leads there.

Lastly, the allusions also play an important role in the play. When Blanche tells Mitch that she is an English teacher, she says, "I attempt to instill a bunch of bobby-soxers and drug-store Romeos with reverence for Hawthorne and Whitman and Poe!" (Williams, 93) The choice of the English writers she mentions here is interesting: Hawthorne lived a life that was solitary to the extreme and suffered acutely from loneliness; Whitman was given to bonding with younger men and was thought to be homosexual; Poe married a young girl who was much younger than he was. Hawthorne, perhaps, reflects her own longing for attention and bondage, while Whitman would signify her brief marriage to Allan Grey. Poe's relationships would symbolize her own last affair with the seventeen-year-old schoolboy, which eventually stopped her from teaching.

The fact that Mitch and Blanche bring home a statuette of Mae West from the amusement park is also interesting. Mae West is known as the sexual icon of the twentieth century. Mitch and

Blanche have only exchanged a good-night kiss once before and act increasingly careful and chaste with one another, but the undercurrent of emotions and sexual desires is very real. Blanche teases Mitch in French, "Will you sleep with me tonight? You do not understand? Ah, what a shame!" Mitch also fumblingly embraces Blanche, saying "Just give me a slap whenever I step out of bounds." (Williams, 108) In this exchange, Mae West is a concise and symbolic figure, representing their repressed desires for each other, but the fact that Mitch is bearing her statuette upside down bodes no good for the future relationship of the couple.

There are many methods through which authors and playwrights communicate subtle implications and ironic undertones. In *Streetcar*, Williams utilizes names, the foremost and most protruding characteristic of an object, to convey different shades of definitions. By manipulating the names of characters, places, and objects of allusion, the playwright subtly shifts the interpretation of the play onto multiple levels, giving the play greater depth and enhancing the message.

Euphemism? or Propaganda?

We all understand why it's done. We've all gone through hard times in the past, and mortifying times as well; we know that sometimes hiding under the thin veneer of deception is much easier than admitting the truth outright.

But sometimes telling lies can be far more detrimental than admitting the truth. Lies, fundamentally built as they are to cover the truth with the illusion of truth, are like spider webs. They are intricate, confusing, sticky, easily tangled, and lure one to one's death.

Even in everyday life the repercussions of lies are bad enough. Sometimes the discovery that the lie was just that- a lie- destroys relationships, reputation, trustworthiness.

But when the repercussions of the lie stretch into societal scale, that's when things start getting ugly in earnest. By ugly we don't just mean "ew-that's-gross ugly," we mean "wow-that's-life-and-death-ugly."

Too harsh? Welcome to the world of propaganda.

When William Zinsser talked about it he called it clutter.

He was talking about *Writing Well*, so I suppose it can't exactly be the same thing, but it still strikes similar at any rate- changing the words to make something sound better than it really is. Propaganda comes from a desire to embellish, a need to conceal.

And ultimately it really is the same thing, especially as it grows more and more deceptive and publicized. When the truth is too keen to face, we weave a shield of jargon and hexasyllabic and heptasyllabic words which we can hide behind. You never tell a lie; you either relay misinformation or commit terminological inexactitude. Where you live can be a depressed socioeconomic area, an economically depressed neighborhood, or a culturally deprived region- anything but a slum. If the government tells you they're utilizing enhanced interrogation methods on potential perpetrators it means they're torturing suspects. The list could go on and on, but ultimately it culminates into one of the most dangerous shields to hide behind: collateral damage, used to refer to innocent deaths.

Propaganda is so detrimental, not only because of the fact that it utilizes deception to deceive the citizens, but also because of the fact that the people come to lose faith in the government that the government will be entirely truthful to them.

The government that does not have a trust-based relationship with its citizens is bound to fail. A government is not something that the people are always obligated to obey. A government has supreme power only under the premise that it will work to get the best for its people. In this case, the government has already failed its duty.

Cat on a Hot Tin Roof

Introduction

I haven't seen Selena lose her composure often, but when she loses it she loses it with a vengeance.

"I don't know what the fuss is all about! Yes, I've changed homerooms. So?"

She stabbed at her rice with a savage fury, the anger plain in her spasmodic motions. I stayed silent, letting her play her temper out. It wasn't only because I was indulging her- I understood her all too well on this point. Last year I had been in a similar position; my class had been notorious for low participation and late homework, and Selena had often acted as my vent as well.

But this year the classes had changed, and it was Selena that was in my shoes and I in Selena's. She took it with better grace than I had, but given the first opportunity to switch homerooms she had done so. Hyunwoo called it smart, Junho called it sensible; I called it taking matters into her own hands. But her classmates called it betrayal. Selena was tired of the racket her switch was causing.

"Lena, it's okay, I understand. But maybe you should talk to the teachers."

The blank look on Selena's face turned into a dawning light of comprehension.

"Oh- Mr. Keating?"

"Yeah, and Ms. Kay."

"Mm, yeah. When do you think?"

I gestured at her dinner tray, the food demolished by her slashing chopsticks.

"After you eat, maybe?"

As it turned out, we didn't have much time after dinner to visit the teachers, so we decided to go after classes. I followed her into the staff room, since I wanted to talk to Ms. Kay about some other assignments in her class, but I covertly watched her as she talked with Mr. Keating. As the conference grew longer they went into a small adjacent room, made expressly for such uses. Mr. Keating left the door ajar and snatches of conversations drifted out- though nothing was clear until the sobs, first small and muted but gradually louder and hysterical.

One of the Korean teachers went in to comfort Selena and Mr. Keating came out, his quick crisp step slow and his face somewhat tired.

"What was all that about?"

He looked at Ms. Kay, not really seeing her, not realizing I was there, and he diagnosed Selena calmly, as only the tired and wise can see the truth.

"She's too frantic, too impatient- she's already worried about college admissions. She's nervous- as nervous as a cat on a hot tin roof…"

Why Maggie the Cat is the Cattiest of Cats

The original version of *Cat on a Hot Tin Roof*, like Williams's best-known play *A Streetcar Named Desire*, was at best a play limning the tragic responses of desperate women facing internal destruction. After director Elia Kazan saw the first draft of *Cat*, however, the play underwent a major metamorphosis. In response to his suggestion that Margaret, the protagonist, be made "more clearly sympathetic to an audience", Williams agreed, saying "…it so happened that Maggie the Cat had become steadily more charming to me as I worked on her characterization," and altered the final act so that the play ended on happier lines. Today the Cat on the Hot Tin Roof that we know is no longer a cat that arches its back for the never-ending heat and pain; it is a cat that sits sedately on a cooled roof, pleased with the outcome.

Maggie is undeniably a cat, but she is the sweetest of cats. She is loving, lonely, forlorn, anxious, and altogether temperamental; she lashes out hard with sharp claws when she is provoked, but when she wants to please she turns soft and gentle and wooing. Williams uses the inflections in Maggie's voice to symbolize her current state of emotions, much as a cat purrs when it is pleased and yowls when it is in pain. In the beginning her voice is "both rapid and drawling··· she intersperses the lines with a little wordless singing" (Williams, 17), and later the playwright describes it as having range and music. When she is begging Brick to love her, her voice becomes "soft and trembling- a pleading child's." (Williams, 50) Maggie, when she is up to please as she is here, has a sweet and songlike voice. In such moods, even a nasty remark hurled against one of her constant tormentors escapes sounding antipathetic but merely "oddly funny, because her eyes constantly twinkle and her voice shakes with laughter which is basically indulgent." (Williams, 22)

Maggie, however, is no mere sweet kitten. When she grows angry her voice grows sharp: in the first quarrel with Brick, both of their voices rise and she has to remind herself and Brick, saying "We mustn't scream at each other." (Williams, 33) Later, in the third act, Maggie's brother-in-law and his wife continue to slander Brick while he is outside having a drink, and she speaks "to herself··· hissingly: Poisons, poisons!" (Williams, 108) Brick, also sick of Maggie's relentless nagging and lovemaking, describes her voice as sounding like she has been "running upstairs to warn somebody that the house was on fire." (Williams, 39)

Maggie also shares another cat-like quality that makes her the ultimate Cat of the story- she might keep up sly appearances, but she never lies to herself. She cheats other people shamelessly, telling Big Daddy that the cashmere gown was a birthday present from Brick and telling the entire company that she is pregnant with Brick's baby. When she and Brick are alone, however, they grow honest almost to the point of brutality. Maggie tells Brick the entire truth of the relationship that went on between Brick's homosexual friend and herself, despite Brick's threats to hit her and even kill her with his crutch.

What, then, gives Maggie the courage to keep on begging, despite Brick's cold refusals and spurns? This lies in how she identifies herself- "Maggie the Cat." She is the Cat, she is alive, and she is clinging onto a hot tin roof that she won't let go of, although she knows that even if she lets go she will land on her four feet uninjured. The tin roof, or at least a part of it, stands for something entirely lacking in Maggie's childhood- wealth. Maggie candidly admits in the first act, "I've been so Goddamn disgustingly poor all my life!" (Williams, 54), and she longs for riches and a pleasant life free from the wretched misery of poverty. When Maggie married Brick Pollitt, she did not only marry Brick himself, she also married into a family owning a twenty-eight thousand acre plantation.

Although Maggie and Brick's relationship is falling apart, Maggie still sinks her claws into the roof in hopes of fulfilling her dream- getting pregnant with Brick's baby, and convincing the dying Big Daddy to hand over the control of the plantation to Brick, his favorite son. Maggie is not the only one who is pursuing this goal, however; her sister-in-law Mae is also in hot pursuit, and Big Daddy describes both of them as looking "as nervous as cats⋯ couple of cats on a hot tin roof." (Williams, 81)

The tin roof, however, is not entirely material; it is also related to abstract desires- most obviously, love. When Brick first tells her to jump off the hot tin roof, he cries, "Do it!- fo' God's sake, do it... Take a lover!" (Williams, 40) The hot tin roof also symbolizes the deteriorating relationship between Maggie and Brick as affairs and drink slowly take over what their original relationship constituted.

Maggie's story, as stated without any embellishment, gives Maggie no dignity and no life. On the surface she seems like the epitome of the calculating wife: after all, she is guilty of having an affair with her husband's friend, but she still tries to cover it up the best she can so that she might have a chance at Big Daddy's fortune. But Maggie has a cattishness that allows her to be admirable. It gives her spring and resiliency, an ability not to give up even when she hears "no" after "no", a hard determination that allows her to carry out well and thoroughly anything she aims to do. So even though Big Daddy says that Mae and Maggie both have the look of cats on a hot tin roof, no one who has read the play would dream of placing the two women on the same level of comparison.

In contrast to the first version of the play Williams wrote, where Maggie and Brick ended on an ambiguous note regarding their relationship, Williams's second version is much kinder to both Maggie and Brick. Brick, in a conversation with Big Daddy, has come to be able to confront the truth, and admires Maggie, whose vivacity of life and desire and drive allows her to face the truth without shame and lead actions that will give the desired results. They end the curtain on a note with near certainty that Maggie and Brick will make love and that Maggie will get pregnant. The cat, then, who clings onto the hot tin roof until the end without giving up, takes the prize.

The Socially Desperate Felines

It's been a long time now since I heard Selena crying in that room- crying like a cat meowing forlornly for the moon, weary and heartsick and desperate. It's been a long time now since I've seen Mr. Keating's face, tired with the symptoms he had already seen in all too many students. But I still remember those memories clearly; I can conjure both up as vividly as if they were happening in front of me all over again, since I've associated both before with so many of my own experiences.

Selena is one of my best friends and I shared a lot of her concerns. Sometimes we raved about teenage nonsense to blow off stress, lulling ourselves into a talking jag only to fall over laughing at the ridiculous things we would say without even thinking, but mostly our conversations built up healthy stress and tension- a paradox, perhaps, but true for all its paradoxity. The stress was healthy since it drove us to limits that we previously hadn't imagined possible, and those limits became heights that we could newly reach. *What colleges can I get into? What should I major in? Where should I apply for early apps? Why are my literature quiz grades so low? What's my GPA this semester? How can I get a higher score on my composition essays? How did you understand enough of what the chemistry teacher was saying to take any notes? What, my math grade fell again?*

But even understanding Selena, I feel that same ennui Mr. Keating must have felt, having seen numerous students go distraught with all the pressures lying so heavily on them. I have no time to do this, no time to do that, trash the reading homework since I have to study for my APs, I don't care if the essay was due today- maybe I'll say the printer was broken and get away with it. Sometimes we don't even remember the definition of having a good time anymore. We've no time at all, good or bad; all we have is study time.

If there's a hot tin roof that we're standing on, some of us are so trained to it, accustomed to it, that we can't even feel the heat rising up on the pads of our paws and toasting them black. And then again some of us have pads so thin and delicate that at the first sign of even remote heat we begin hopping around like mad until we finally propel ourselves off the surface, just barely a few seconds after the pain starts. We all of us are cats, and even if we jump we still land on the ground mostly intact; but the ones that jump don't get the prize, and the ones who don't jump without training themselves burn up completely. It's survival of the fittest; Darwin knew what he was talking about- except, in social Darwinism, the laws of fair play fly straight out the window.

But we stand there, and we wait, training ourselves to the heat, baking in the hot sun, and digging our claws into the tin, until the rain clouds blow over the sweltering sun and grace us with the drops of coolness and inspiration which recharge us with the energy to start the process all over again. Because, truth be told, this cycle never really ends- after college there's always graduate school, or work; and once having gotten there, there are promotions to worry about; and even after that another list continues endless.

Though not many of us know exactly why we're all standing on the hot tin roof- for whatever reason- except to maybe boast that we have stood the tin roof, and that we have black paws to prove it- the few cats who go to the edge of the roof to peek out at the view the roof provides, know why they stand there. The tragedy lies in the fact that the majority of the cats are clinging on for some undefinable reason, but don't have the patience or the energy to peer out and see what it's worth.

Macbeth

Introduction

There was a time, during my sophomore AP crash period, when my class fell in love with AP subject-related pickup lines.

I understood Donghyun when he started cracking up over some AP Psychology pickup lines. After all, he was studying Freud. Their entire topic was built on sexual orientation and repression.

What can you expect?

But Selena was a different matter. She was taking AP US History at the time.

"Wouldn't it be funny," she asked dreamily, "if there were pickup lines for US History?"

"Don't even think about it, Selena," I groaned.

But obviously there were more people out there in the world like her, since we Googled "AP US History pickup lines" and we found a surprising number of hits. We huddled over her iPhone, glancing down the lines, and then the same one caught our eye. We froze, then-

"Oh- my- GOD!" we shrieked. "Oh- my- God-"

"What? What is it?" Junho came sauntering over to us, and when Selena held out her phone, he stared at it blankly for a while before cracking up and moving away, slowly shaking his head.

But soon the entire class was caught up in the rage, and for a while everyone remotely interested in US History was howling over those lines every break. Selena, bless her heart, even made up a few. They weren't too bad.

Then the trend moved onto World History. Then Chemistry. The list went on and on.

I believe AP Calculus and AP Statistics remained comparatively unscathed.

But there was another subject that remained untouched, except for just one pickup line, and that was AP Literature. It really was because I was the only one in my class taking it. Most of the class was worrying over their AP Language; they would take Lit in their junior year.

But the entire AP-pickup fad was in its dying stages, and I was discussing the AP Lit FRQ questions with Selena, when Soohye ran up to us with a large smile on her face.

"I've got an AP Lit pickup line," she giggled. "Do you want to hear it?"

"Sure."

She whispered: "I'll wait for you, baby, until Birnam Wood comes to Dunsinane Hill."

We looked at each other and howled.

The Macbeths of Today

I first read *Macbeth* when I was a middle schooler, in the same way I had read *Julius Caesar* and *Antony and Cleopatra*- for fun. I first read *Julius Caesar* because my sister was studying it in her own English class, and there was something indefinable about *Brutus, et tu?* that captivated me and began me on a Shakespeare-reading jag. But I didn't actually study *Macbeth* until very recently, when the AP Lit course in my new school chose to study that book; and sitting in on one of the classes as Student Aid I was delighted to read along and follow the diverse interpretations of Shakespeare I had first become weaned to during my sophomore year. Admittedly we had studied a somewhat boring history play then, *Henry IV*, but it definitely trained me to read and appreciate Shakespeare without having a NoFear Shakespeare[4] on the monitor in front of me.

When I first reread *Macbeth* I remembered I had far preferred the

---

4) A site that places Shakespearean dialogue next to its modern-day translation for the benefit of students having a hard time understanding Elizabethan English.

beauty in *Romeo and Juliet*, or even the desperation of characters in *Othello*, to the cold and calculating world of Macduff and Macbeth. But then so many of my friends in Korea had loved *Macbeth* so well, that I decided there must be something to it that I hadn't seen.

There had been something I hadn't seen. In fact, there had been many things. For one, I'd loved studying the poetry unit on scansion when I was preparing for AP Lit, but I didn't realize until I re-read the play that one of the best examples of trochaic tetrameter was that famous witch chant from *Macbeth*- "Double, double, toil and trouble, Fire burn and cauldron bubble." More importantly, over the subtle theme of witchcraft that had so scared me the first time I read the play, I was able to appreciate the keen play Shakespeare had wrought on a shortcoming shared by all mankind.

It is a question battled over even today, if man forges his own future, or if he merely thinks he does so and in truth he only follows the lines drawn out by some hand of an unknown Divine Power, far above us. Thus works that deal with the battle between Man and Fate appeal to us with a constant unchanging appeal regardless of time, unaltered from whatever power they originally owned in the time frames of their creation. And since humanity oftener than not feels a need to assert itself over powers of either the natural world or the supernatural world there are frequent works reflecting the process of humanity forging his own fate, whether for good or for bad.

Similarly *Macbeth* struggles on the fine borderline of the power balance between fortune's capricious tricks and man's overt ambition. Whereas other works of literature often introduce mediators between fortune and man so that man can gain some other type of advantage- such as witchery and magic- Macbeth's witches only serve as an earthly face for fate, and he himself is only given the weapon of ambition with which to fight the heavens. Macbeth, the titular character as well as the main character, becomes nothing more than a vessel holding his desire and obeying its call. The play ends with the main character having become so blinded to, and drowned in, his lust for power that the reader can feel no pity for him when he at last falls to his death.

I think that's why I really didn't like it when I was young. It was an age when stories were supposed to end happily, as of yet; and tragedies were supposed to be great raging things of love like *Romeo and Juliet*. It was an age when I only appreciated the books that I saw perfect ideals drawn in, an age when I didn't appreciate the books that I would come to empathize with. I didn't realize that one day I would re-read this and see my own self reflected in the blood on Macbeth's hands that all Neptune's seas would not be able to wash off. I would only return to weep with the thane of Cawdor as I reaped the results of my own ambition and desire.

My friends, who had learned before me that the beauty of books was in how sympathetic they were, had realized their own shortcomings earlier than I had, and could look on *Macbeth*, both the person and the play, with a kinder eye and an appreciation for the keen truth.

I don't know the impression most people get when they're labeled "Asian", but for me it's never been too positive. I don't think I'm being oversensitive about it. Not really. Of course there are those matter-of-fact scenarios when people say, "Yes, she's Asian." It's the truth, and a rather obvious one at that- dark hair, dark eyes; yes, open your eyes. I am Asian and I am proud of it.

But there are those other times, those other moments, when being Asian carries wholly different meanings, and these are the instants that seem negative and hurtful. I've attended international schools for seven years, and I've spent another two in a quasi-international surrounding. I've heard the discriminatory comments often and I know the implications well. I also know that most of the time the discrimination is teasing, and that if it's hurtful it's unintentionally hurtful. The fact remains that it is hurtful.

For example: some of my blue-eyed friends exclaim, "You're Asian! Of course you're good at math." Well, I'm not. Live with it. And then often I hear different terms that mean the same thing, used both as praises and chastisements. When my friends tire of studying, and they want to chill for an hour or so and they want me to chill with them, they whine, "Han Bin, you're being so dull and Korean. Let's just have fun for one day." When finals are coming up and I'm busy cramming my head with Biology-related paraphernalia, classmates laugh and say that although I seem like a Twinkie[5] for most of the time, test periods prove just how Korean I am. I love being Korean, more than I love being Asian, and I love the diligence and the social pressure that comes with being born into Asian communities. But I don't like being stereotyped. I don't want to be seen as simply another generic nerd, yet another Korean bookworm when I know that the reasons and the passion for my pursuit of dreams is unique and fueled with a powerfully personal longing. I hate having my desires degraded to the level of a simple nerd's mechanical actions.

Because that is what has mainly become how we Asians are seen, now, for those last three years spanning our high school life; study-obsessed freaks that have been grinded into a machine and shoved into a mold that plops us out onto a conveyor belt, all ready to be gift-wrapped and sold. When we take a test the results must necessarily be one hundred percent full score. The ideas are widespread, universal. I don't think it's even the question

---

5) A term, slightly derogatory, used to refer to Asian-Americans: white on the inside and Asian on the outside

of the parents pushing, spurring on the initially unwilling but still obediently docile children, like Amy Chua's *Battle Hymn of the Tiger Mother* suggests. Nowadays most students are the ones that push themselves into the molds for better results. The mother often merely watches and encourages while the children race themselves to unchallenged heights.

And since this rage is self-initiated the battle for the better and the best, inevitably, follows competition. After all, the best can only be given to one person. HIGHEST SCORER, one certificate reads. And other trophies are labeled, BEST VIOLINIST. MOST FLUENT SPEAKER. The list goes on and on. And everyone strives to make at least one mark, one place that they can establish as their own.

Sometimes the competition ends gently, with friendly jibes and encouraging rivalry, but most times it rages horribly. I remember something that happened when I was a sophomore in Korea, a little incident that taught me just how ferocious this fight could get. Now, I am a good note-taker on the whole, and I take pride in rewriting and organizing neatly. Once I was talking with my friends before getting ready for the next class, and about two minutes before the bell rang I went to my locker to get my textbook; and lo and behold the textbook was gone!

My horror may well be imagined. I searched my desk; my laptop bag; my bag; it was nowhere. I ran to the teacher and begged him to excuse my lack of preparation, and he laughed understandingly and told me he thought it would turn up before the end of the day somehow. Such things had often happened before during test-periods.

During the dinner hour I trotted outside with Jaemin for a quick meal. On the way back we stopped by a printing shop to print out an essay that was due that night; stacked on top of the copier, I saw my textbook and a copied set of my notes. I quietly took my textbook but left the stack of notes, and when I later saw a classmate peering over them, I let him be.

The memory of those nightmarish minutes remains with me yet. But I was struck comparatively mildly. A few of my friends have actually had their books stolen, before; and they had no choice but to buy a new one and recopy the notes down.

Now it's come to the state that all of us Koreans are being seen as present-day Macbeths, people so greedy for superiority that they would stop at nothing. And if we have not all become such present-day Macbeths enough of us have acted similarly enough for a universal stereotype to be developed and applied. Some of us even try to just fit the stereotype and embark on a purposeless path of competition. Thus, whichever case it is, we come to constitute a society of Macbeths. Admittedly none of us quite commit murder for grades; but that was a time when warfare was rampant, and now it is a time when studying is rampant. Our study methods are the daggers and swords of today, and stopping other people from studying is no less underhanded than midnight murders.

The thing to reflect now, then, is if we really want to continue this path. A large part of this study craze has been tied irrevocably into our culture. It is the Korean mindset to be diligent, to work hard, and to gain prosperity, and I am by no means saying that it is bad. But is this- this endless competitive series of moral and mental catfights- the only way to fulfill what our culture deems honorable goals? I think not. At least we should be able to escape, in one way or another, the shortcomings of Macbeth.

Part Three

Life in Life

: Social Analysis

The Glass Menagerie

Introduction

"I'm going to opium dens! Yes, opium dens, dens of vice and criminals' hang-outs, Mother. I've joined the Hogan gang, I'm a hired assassin, I carry a tommy-gun in a violin case! I run a string of cat-houses in the Valley! They call me Killer, Killer Wingfield. I'm leading a double life, a simple, honest warehouse worker by day, by night a dynamic czar of the underworld, Mother. I go to gambling casinos, I spin away fortunes on the roulette table! On those occasions they call me- El Diablo!"

"More emotion, Hyunwoo! That's too weak!"

"Mr. Henderson, this is a memory play!"

"We are in the middle of a very painful memory! Everything is clearer, doubly clearer, than reality! Good God, kid, what type of devil speaks like that?"

Hyunwoo wriggled his eyebrows at me, his eyelids hooded heavily with sarcasm, and I giggled. Only Mr. Henderson would think of invoking God's name in trying to encourage someone to act more 'accurately devilish.'

"Ms. Kim, perhaps you would like to give it a try?"

I blushed a bright red, stammering out a hasty denial of sorts, but Mr. Henderson, if sacrilegious, was definitely persistent.

"Go on, girl. You were laughing at Hyunwoo."

"Not at Hyunwoo, sir, at-"

I stopped, horrified at myself. Mr. Henderson saw my face and chuckled.

"At me, I suppose. Here, I'll read a section, then you try seeing how you can do it. Fair?"

I nodded and curled up in a little ball on the beanbag chair. Mr. Henderson's satisfying voice rang out in a strong baritone through the classroom. For a few seconds, the students forgot his sarcastic side and watched him, entranced, as his captivating reading drew us in.

"In Spain there was revolution. Here there was- only shouting and confusion. In Spain there was- Guernica. Here- there were disturbances of labor, sometimes pretty violent, in otherwise peaceful cities such as Chicago, Cleveland, Saint Louis. This is the social background of the play."

A long pause. Then softly-

"This play is memory."

The whistling applause drew us all back to reality.

The Significance of a Memory Play
: The Glass Menagerie

When I was in Shenyang, a state in the far north of China, I lived in a tall apartment complex with a luxurious bedroom and a giant living room, and gilded elevators with ornate lights that reminded the rider faintly of the stunning majesty of the Titanic. Or at least that's the silent breathtaking pleasure with which I always boarded the elevator, waiting for the soft green lights to pulse and the chime to ring out soft and clear. Until the elevator completed its smooth ascent to the eleventh floor, I would stand under the soft incandescent orange lights and study my reflection in the mirrors of the walls and the polished lacquer of the doors.

At the same time, one of my best friends, Jinwook, lived in a dilapidated townhouse where the paint was peeling off in patches. When winter came the half-tar, half-sand roads regularly disappeared under a ten-inch blanket of snow and the roads were not cleared until the first brave car came plundering through, treading the new snow with a mixture of trepidation and anticipation. Pedestrians had the Hobson's choice of breaking a path for themselves to their respective houses, or slipping and sliding on the perilously slippery icy pavement.

Sometimes the main door wouldn't open since it was frozen shut at the cracks, and then we would have to tug together at the door. If it didn't give way we kept on trying until more people eventually came to our aid, and if it did give way- suddenly, in the way cracking ice always gives way- we invariably fell tumbling over, giggling, into the heavy snow behind us. Then we dusted ourselves off the best we could and tripped up the stairs, leaving pools of melting snow on the frigid cement steps. They froze there to serve as a reminder to the next person, coming up or going down, that winter was inescapable. Often the victims were us.

I studied English with Jinwook every Saturday in the church annex, which was the flat right under his own, and so we went over to his home very frequently. Sometimes we ran up for a cup of water or a biscuit to nibble on, and sometimes we ran up to get something printed; and at such times I would make faces at the full-length mirror embedded into the door as he crouched over the computer monitor. Once, I was studying the reflection of my face under the lights, as I did whenever I boarded my elevator, and I thought vaguely that his bedroom would perhaps be double its size. I never told him. He knew.

Our homes were too far apart for either one of us to see the other without the use of a car, so he rarely came over to my home, but in seventh grade he started coming over more regularly. With every visit he visibly shook under the turbulent gusts of wind that buffeted and disturbed his sensitive mindset. They would be enough to estrange him from me for weeks at a time. But then he came back to my side, as if nothing had happened. One of Jinwook's greatest flaws- but it was my favorite part about him, all the same- was that he was sensitive. And something admirable about him, in any case, was that he tortured his own sensitivity by forcing himself to face the truth. It was no easy job for a boy barely thirteen years old. Even at seventeen years of age it's still difficult.

Once he stayed over rather late on Friday night, and his sister Somang and I had collapsed on the bed giggling over a funny story, but he stood with his hand against the large French window and his face fixed into a scowl. I stopped laughing and watched as his long fingers slowly clenched into a fist.

"Are you alright?" I asked.

"No," he said in a low voice, and as he turned I thought I saw the reflections of the city lights swimming in his dark brown eyes. But he blinked and the pools of light disappeared, so I pressed no further. By the next day he had written a short composition that he didn't want to show me in the beginning.

"It's short," he muttered, and he pulled his notebook away.

His response surprised me for two reasons. First of all, Jinwook knew that I knew his English was even worse than my Chinese, and if he had written only a short composition in lieu of an essay- or if he hadn't written any at all- he would grin at me and tell me that he was sorry. I always laughed over it. I couldn't help it. His candidness had the shining quality of the barefaced pleasure of children, which always invites others to laugh at their adorable simplicity and boldness.

Secondly, Jinwook never wrote short compositions. He complained that short compositions barely ever got an idea across. My mother, whom Jinwook already called Aunt Agatha, had tried to break him of the habit, but Jinwook was a born writer and a born orator whose quick tongue often fell behind the pace of his quicker thoughts. Thus the only days on which he brought short works were days during the finals prep period or when he was sick.

The thoughts flashed by as I looked at him. "Jinwook?"

He glanced quickly at me, then he slowly let his grip loose. "Don't- don't get hurt. I didn't mean it at you."

I gently took the notebook from him and it flipped open of its own accord to the last page. He had spent a lot of time on it. He had written one line, then crossed it out, then another two lines, then crossed it out, and this frustrated routine continued for over half the page. At the bottom there were three lines, heavily scoring the paper, and when I passed my hand over the marks he had made I could feel the weight of the anger he had concentrated into the tip of his pencil and pressed down with.

'Her house is wealth. It is not wealthy. It is wealth. Wealth is the rooms, the table, the chandeliers, the bed, the city lights.'

'My house is poverty. The desk is small. The bed is hard. The stars are my city lights.'

Eight simple sentences that conveyed an infinity of pain and sorrow. I longed to put my hand on his shoulder, to say something to comfort him, but he was playing with the whiteboard marker and studiously avoiding looking at me. Wordlessly I closed the notebook and gave it back to him, and I set Cecilia to read her own composition out loud. As she stumbled over the words she had written Jinwook looked at me and gave me a small smile. *I'm sorry*, he mouthed.

Now Jinwook is no longer here and the only thing that remains with me is the memories that I shared with him: the funny, confident, straightforward boy he used to be, and how reticent and shy a creature he gradually became. Since I first saw him when he was still young and careless and unafraid to speak his thoughts, he remained like that to me for most of the time, but it took some time to lure him out every time I saw him. In the first minutes I would see a new stranger lurking behind the face of the boy I had known. The stranger looked out with fear and trepidation out of the clear dark eyes that had once held cheerful courage and fearless laughter.

It's a very long story about a person that seems to have no

substantial connection to *The Glass Menagerie*, but for me, Jinwook was the first person I thought of when I read about Laura Wingfield.

It's weird that I think of Jinwook first. In many ways it should have been Somang, Jinwook's little sister, whom I should have been reminded of, since Somang is sweeter and more timid than Jinwook in many ways. Somang hated strangers, and when someone she didn't know or she didn't like asked her a question, she withdrew completely into her own world. But when she did open up to someone she liked, she opened up completely, a totally new identity that budded into a flower with brilliant splashes of color. Jinwook gradually withdrew from even the people he had once known and loved, increasingly unsure of himself and what he wanted to do.

Of course, Laura suffers more acutely than Jinwook did. She has more factors adding to her discomfort and shyness. Laura is slightly crippled, despite her mother's efforts to deny the fact, and when she walks it must necessarily be with the aid of a leg brace. But a bigger problem is her shyness, which makes her shy away from the outside world. Her insecurity about herself is partly due to her malformed leg- when she was in high school she quit choir since she felt that the sound of the metal brace on her leg was too conspicuous and loud- but this same feeling of discomfort influences all future aspects of her life: Laura stops going to Rubicam's Business College due to her tremendous shyness, and seems quite content with the prospect of being an old maid. Her fear of having to interact with people outside her tightly-knit community of mother and brother is greater than the fear of being viewed as a social failure. Her shyness becomes as crippling a factor to her real life as her actual limp, since it becomes an impediment in how she approaches people and indeed enters social gatherings.

If *The Glass Menagerie* was only a story of the past or the far future it would have remained a story I would have loved and appreciated, and I would have oohed and aahed over the keen portrayal of emotions, and I would have fallen in love with the way Williams mixed the factors of a memory play inside *Glass* in order to give the characters more life and more vivacity without demeaning the factors of Laura's shyness thereof. But the story was too close to me for me to view so placidly: it was a story I had witnessed too recently, in Jinwook's life, and a story that I was sure would be continuing elsewhere, for someone else's best friend. She would feel as helpless as I had, watching her friend recede into a shell, no matter how much she would try to pull him out.

I think it is necessary to explain that today the crippling factor of poverty is worse than any other possible flaw, not only for the increased importance it holds in today's society but for its very universality. Compared to the past it holds increased importance because it is like a heavy chain that can stop a character from becoming what he might become, blocking potential and possibility alike, since it cripples the confidence of a character. The definition of a character as given by his income bracket has become definitive. And as capitalism becomes more and more developed, many societies have marked an increase in their Gini coefficient, a growing disparity of wealth between the very rich and the very poor. As distribution of wealth becomes more and more stilted, and as some benefit more, there are necessary some that must benefit less.

Throughout the years, Laura Wingfield's argument lost strength and persuasiveness as cripples became more and more easily healed, and pains of all types grew to the frequency where they were seen as everyday. They lost the impact they once had. But perhaps Laura's agony, deriving from her shyness and inability to act boldly, has manifested itself through her crippled leg, and the real pain Williams is trying to communicate behind her pain of being crippled physically, is the pain of being crippled socially.

Thus Jinwook's pain relates the same flow of emotions that Laura first felt: an intense need to hide when everyone else's conditions seem so supremely above one's own pathetic state. To the universal reader both examples provide insight into the pain that people suffer from with the shortcomings that are not due to their talent but instead to birth, and teaches us to empathize with it. To me- and to everyone else that has suffered with a friend growing more and more crippled- it is a desperate issue that must be addressed and healed.

The Pearl

The Pearl in the Slums

The first work of Steinbeck's that I read was *Of Mice and Men*. I read it when I was in tenth grade, right during the midterms' crash period. I sometimes read books during those crash periods- when I felt as if memorizing one more thing would send my brain spiraling down a black hole, those thin books that could be read in the space of an hour were welcome and cathartic. *Of Mice and Men* was a heartbreakingly warm, poignant tale that stimulated me to study even more after I got back home late at night, nigh eleven o'clock.

Right after the midterms were over I thought I recalled seeing Steinbeck in my bookshelf, so I went and dug the book up. *The Pearl* was even thinner than *Of Mice and Men* so I sat down straight away and read it through. While I read it I was reminded of a certain group of kids I had taught just until a month ago, when I set them on vacation while I studied for my tests.

In the very heart of Seoul, among the tall skyscrapers and the busy eight-lane roads and the buildings that flaunt their blinding lights amidst the peaceful brightness of city nights, there is a little town where no streetlamps light the perilous untarred roads, where the houses are plastic boards that have been planted into the ground in a pathetic attempt to define property, and where the roofs of the wealthier are grey boards of slate and more often than not are thick pieces of tarp fixed to the scanty infrastructure of the house by rocks and cords of fraying rope.

It's the last of the economically depressed neighborhoods in Seoul, the politicians say in their well-bred voices, but it's hard to realize it when you just hear it the way it's said. It's only when you're actually striding down those paths with the dust rising hot and gritty in the summer heat waves, and the cheap shine of the tarp flashing ferociously, that you feel it to be what it really is: a slum.

Then you look up to glare at the hot sun and you realize that what you actually thought to be the sun was only the reflection off the paneled windows of the Tower Palace, home to Seoul's elite. It looms in the distance, cool and collected with its many windows and metallic beam, unaware of the sweltering shacks sagging dangerously with the heat not too far away. And then you feel the poignancy of it all.

I've walked these streets many times, with students ranging anywhere from second grade to seventh grade. I don't think I've ever picked a pricklier batch of roses. It takes a long time for them to bud or to bloom, and until then, all you can feel are the stings from their thorns. For the first few weeks they look at you with distaste just barely hidden under their mutters of "Yes'm" or "No'm". Hearing an actual backlash from them is a good sign- it shows you're getting somewhere with them. That's step two. Talking back. After you alternate scolding and tolerating for about a month then they finally start doing their homework. That's where the learning actually starts.

But like all roses they have their buds and they have their blooms. As difficult as it is to keep from crying, at times, when they whip out one of those mean comments that they actually don't know how much it hurts, the confidence that they later grant you is flattering. Many of the students that came to study didn't come for the sake of learning whatever I was teaching, whether it was violin or English: they came to socialize and have a fun time. If they didn't think that they would have a fun time, they didn't come; but once they liked you sufficiently to come then they would do whatever you told them to do without complaining. They liked to ask me what I had studied in school that week, and if I told them in English and set them to figure it out, or if I told them that I would maybe tell them if they could finish playing a short piece by the end of the lesson, then they did it.

They all hated pity, and I tried not to give it to them. They had experienced too much contempt under the guise of pity that all types of condolences immediately brought them on their guard. At the first sight of "Oh, you poor darlings!" they would retreat somewhere deep into themselves and present a veneer that was not easy to penetrate. Even the fourth, fifth graders already knew what to say and what not to say in front of others, and they carefully disguised their words so that their school friends would not know that they lived in the little town by the mountains. Only the second graders ever spoke frankly about their living conditions. I remember one, a little darling we called Baby, who tugged shyly at my hand not too long after I had made friends with her.

"Teacher, can I be absent tomorrow?"

"Why, Baby?"

Her eyes were big and clear in her chubby little face. "My daddy's going to the city to get coal tomorrow, so I need to stay home and take care of Mommy."

This town still used coal- it was a fact that surprised me every time I saw the used briquettes lying discarded on the corners dividing the streets. Baby's father was the leading coal merchant of the town, a big man who had flashed me a good-natured grin the first time I walked Baby home. Winter was here, so business would be booming, and I thought how his smile would be like a flash of white among the dark coal. But Baby's mother was a pale, weak, frail woman who only coughed fretfully to greet her daughter when the door opened, and when I lingered at the doorway to bid Baby goodbye she had cried, "Mercy, Baby, remember my cold and shut the door!"

All these thoughts were still flashing through my head when Hyejin snapped, "Baby, how many times do I have to tell you not to say that?"

Baby opened her large eyes even wider, looking scared and bewildered, and the blush of pink slid from her cheeks to be replaced by a pale white. "Wh-what did I say?"

"That your daddy was going to get coal. Say your daddy has a business trip tomorrow- that's not a lie, is it? And it sounds better."

"What's wrong with coal?" Baby defended in what I was later to learn was a highly defensive gesture for her.

"Rich people don't use coal! They have electric heaters that heat up their homes! Coal's only something you talk about in this town."

"But we're in this town," Baby objected. Her lower lip trembled, and Hyejin, the nasty little spitfire, the scary, cold, catlike girl who had taken so long to win over, softened and reached out and hugged her with her long spindly arms.

"Don't cry, Baby. Don't cry. I'm sorry. It's okay here. But don't say it anywhere else. If you say it in front of your friends they never look at you the same way again. Baby Kim, they say, pointing their fingers. Baby Kim lives in a small ugly house that uses coal."

Not too long after that I was trotting along the cold frosty paths with Jungmin, a mature sixth grader eager to start middle school, and we were speculating how nice and warm the small classroom would be after these horrendous streets. Jungmin was the student that I was closest to and she opened up to me in a rare fit of honesty.

"My father should stay in some Saturday," she remarked, kicking the snow as she walked. "It's getting too cold."

"Are you worried he'll get frostbite?" I smiled.

"No, it's just- the boards of the walls are cracking open and the snow and the wind are seeping in. He needs to fix them up. Right now we can barely feel the warmth from the coal."

"Oh," I said quietly.

"Mmm," she grunted. "And the privy's frozen over. It's horrendous."

"Privy?" I asked her cautiously. She nodded grimly. "Privy. You know, outdoor bathroom."

Just then the shrieks that reached us from the small schoolhouse made us run, all conversation forgotten. When we wrenched open the doors we saw Hyejin and Sungwoo fighting over a bag of wheat crackers. Baby was crying in the corner.

"What's happening?" I asked in my sternest voice. Hyejin and Sungwoo froze, then they started hurling accusations at each other.

"I'm the one that said let's buy this one!" "But you didn't pay for it!"

"Well, neither did you!"

I stopped their quibbling. "Who paid for it?"

Hyejin pointed at Sungwoo. "He stole it!"

I stared, aghast, at Sungwoo. "You stole it?" He looked at me sullenly and I saw the beginnings of his old defensiveness creeping up on him, like a suit of armor that he was beginning to strap on. "Sungwoo, I won't blame you. I won't tell you on anyone either. But can you tell me why?"

There was no answer for a while, then he muttered, "I was hungry."

"Did you have lunch?" I asked. He shook his head, and his head hung even lower. I waited for him to speak to me, signaling Jungmin and the rest to unpack their violins. When the rest of the classroom was safely occupied with the twanging of strings he spoke again, barely audibly. "Can you come with me?"

Curious now, I went with him outside the schoolhouse back into the cold, and we walked for a while in silence. He stopped at his house, which was yet unlit, and I remembered that he and his father lived alone. He quickly slipped in and brought out a cardboard box, the type new shoes come in.

Under the lid was a little sparrow that had broken its leg.

There was nothing to do but to hug the little boy tight, and soon he was crying, the cardboard box cradled in his arms shuddering as he wept into my black coat.

The tale of Kino and Juana cannot be identical to these kids, wonderful kids whom I still treasure in my memory, but there is an underlying theme that is all too similar: the beauty and the innocence of the destitute that invariably becomes destroyed with age and experience. These kids might not be the gentlest, most soft-spoken kids I know, but among their own they were the kindest and the most loving. The fierce protection which each felt for another was equivalent to Kino's battle for his family, and the song of their loving as loud.

I read the story again and I think that the greatest reason Kino's family was pushed out into danger and evil was due to the dishonesty of the traders that tried to cheat Kino in the beginning.

We do not ignore Kino's wrongdoings. The fact that Kino came to value selfishness above community, or wealth above life, is inexcusable, and his eyes were definitely blinded by the wealth he had newly accumulated. If Kino had been the person he had been before he discovered the pearl, Kino would have let himself be robbed of the pearl, giving his fate up to the heavens in his classically admirable phlegmatic way.

But if he had let himself be robbed many would have praised

him for being idealistically righteous, whereas many would have condemned him as being practically foolish. His longing for wealth and a better life is an inevitable response considering the magnitude of the discovery he made. With Kino, the wrongs he committed are balanced with the wrongs that he didn't commit, and for the most part the reader can be generous in their judgment of Kino. He is easily justifiable.

The wealthy who tried to cheat Kino even of his once-in-a-lifetime discovery, are not so much. The dealers knew fully well that the pearl was worth more than what they had asked for, and if Kino's own appraisement of the pearl was not quite accurate it could not have been further off than the appraisement of the dealers: "as Kino thrust the pearl out of sight⋯ they knew they had played too hard; they knew they would be disciplined for their failure." (Steinbeck, 52) From then on starts Kino's downfall, in earnest, as thieves try to steal the pearl from him on his journey to the capital.

Even now there are too many people that try to drag down the values of pearls in the lives of the financially deficient. Every time one of my students is looked down by a classmate, whether by action, word, or thought- she is being maltreated by the dealers all over again. She is being pushed to more and more dangerous boundaries. Lying was already a commonplace happening among the fifth- and sixth-graders, even when I taught them, and the kids told me that not many students from the town were able to stick to the path of the right and the good until high school. Their older brothers smoked, their older sisters drank, and for all of them, skipping school was as commonplace as going to it.

It saddens me to think that often we act as cruelly as we do without even thinking about it. When we think about the coals and the privies that these students have to use every day, there is a faint contempt that cannot help but be mixed into how we treat them. When they act up and don't obey what I wish them to do, even I- who have been so constantly exposed to the pain the students feel in response to any type of stereotyping or disdain- think, well, what can you expect from these students. It's something that we need to constantly awaken ourselves to, stimulate ourselves to remember- that they need the same kind treatment that the rest of society gets. That they need more.

The week after Sungwoo had showed me the sparrow and wiped his tears on my coat, I went to the shop Sungwoo said he had taken the bag of crackers from to pay for it. The shopkeeper was a short fat lady of whom I uncharitably thought that she would look much better if she smiled instead of frowning. I smiled for her instead.

"There was a little boy here, last week, who took a bag of wheat crackers?" I asked.

"Yes, he did, and scampered away with it too, the little villain!" she screeched. "And a little girl who ran away with him. Both of them were too fast for my legs. No doubt both of them are from that terrible slum village, right across two streets!"

Mentally thankful that I had refused to let Sungwoo come with me, I ignored her tirade and silently held out some money. She looked at me curiously. "Are you paying for it? Why?"

"Yes- I'm his sister," I replied curtly. It wasn't a lie; he called me sister, and I liked to think him my brother. But the lady looked at me for a while, and then she leaned back in her seat, chuckling.

"No, you're not his sister, not by a long shot. You don't belong there. But you know him, and you're paying for him, aren't you?"

She did look a lot better when she smiled. I nodded.

"Well, the world needs more people like you, and that's a fact. I suppose if you can pay for a little boy, then I can go without that much."

She handed the money back to me, and I stared at her incredulously. There was a lot more hope to this world than I had expected to find.

"Was he hungry?" she asked abruptly. I shook my head.

"No, he was trying to feed a sick sparrow."

"God bless the boy!" the woman sighed as she turned to the next man waiting in line.

Frankenstein

Introduction

I've said once before that I was a born "skimmer", and it really shows in my reading habits- most of the books I love are the ones that I first read when I was young, and came back to later, to re-read into love. The same applies to *Frankenstein*.

I will admit that *Frankenstein* was never a book that I had really loved. The content is a little too Gothic to be that. But when I was in high school I came back to read it- twice. The first time was because one of the passages came out in an AP Literature prep test, and I liked the excerpt so much that I hunted up the full version and read it through. And the second time I read it was right after I read it through the first time. The book was just so good. It is a book that is wonderful and inspirational, since it is a work of ageless horror as well as a work of youthful creativity. Youthful creativity! Do I dare?

I remember once, I believe it was during Ms. Lowett's class, that we were assigned a creative writing piece, and the entire class set up a howl when she assigned a five-page story due the very next day.

Junho took charge of leading the complaints.

"Aw, Ms. Lowett, you've got to be kidding us. We need time for this."

"I didn't hear you complain when I assigned you a seven-page research paper last week," Ms. Lowett smilingly reminded us. "Was it because you could just take one of your old papers and re-stitch it together?"

"Oh, goodness heavens, no!" Junho looked the very picture of innocence, and since I had witnessed him in the very act of slapping together his research paper two hours before the due time I couldn't help but laugh at his comical duplicity. "But- but- we're too young to write stories. If we want to write good stories we need to have wisdom, wisdom that comes from age. Do you really want to spend your precious time grading mediocre work?"

Ms. Lowett laughed. "If you want to spend the next thirty minutes arguing over this, I won't complain, but if you have to spend the night up don't you dare tell me that I didn't give you enough time for this. I think I'm being too nice. You should see Mr. Parry's deadlines."

She walked to the door amidst a clamor of complaints and wails, and as she opened the door she turned around and gave the class a mischievous smile. "By the way, kids, Mary Shelley was eighteen when she wrote *Frankenstein*. I expect work of equal quality by tomorrow."

The entire class shut up like magic.

Becoming Frankenstein

The car ride is a pleasant one, except for the fact that the Jeep is high and it jolts with the slight bumps on a road mostly evenly tarred. My parents have made this into something like a picnic for me, buying burgers and chicken wings to eat on the way; and after a long stretch of junior life the trip is all too welcome. When I was young I slept during long car rides, since even then I was easily susceptible to carsickness, but now these fleeting hours are all too precious and I grab at them eagerly. The houses and buildings outside the windows disappear as rapidly as the burgers we are gobbling down and soon we are speeding down the highway, munching at the last of the chicken wings.

The road stretches out for a colorlessly long time and the only thing imbuing the trip with hue is the bright chatter that bounces back and forth between the front seats and the back. It is winter. Against the grey sky and the grey air and the grey tar of the road, the bright blue and the stark black of our padded coats vividly stand out.

The colors that splotch the monochromatic scene quickly turn into queasiness. Soon the waves of nausea swamping the back seat are like the gusts of wintry wind howling across the barren land. I sit crouched, huddled, a little ball of misery at the mercy of this grey sea.

But my mother says, *We're nearly there*, and the Jeep slows as we peer across the ashy stretch of tar with so many country roads leading off from the side. The nausea slowly ebbs out. *Which one*, my father asks, and my mother says *I'll know it when I see it*. And so we go down the road, chugging along steadily, and I peer down every road to wonder if this is the one. But my mother says nothing.

It might be this one, she presently says, and the Jeep slows down as we get ready to turn down the side- but at the last moment my mother says no, and we drive on. Down the asphalt road a white plastic picket fence divides the cars coming from the ones going, so in the case that we make a mistake turning around will be hard. But my mom doesn't seem to worry that we might pass the magic road altogether and have to turn around and search again. Distantly I remember a fear I used to have when I was very young, and my heart jumps queerly at the distasteful trepidation: if the car was supposed to make a turn just here, and my father missed the right moment, then we would have no choice but to go on searching for a place to turn, forever and forever into the horizon···

Just then my mother says *Yes*, at the mouth of a thin path that seems no different from any of the others, and my father jerks the wheel, pulling the Jeep clattering down a grey country road.

The road is calm and placid, with the red bricks of houses dusty but friendly from age. The neatly aligned rows of houses remind me of-

My hometown used to be like this when I was a little boy, my father remarks, and my mom adds, *All country towns were*. And I realize that the friendliness steeped into the very bricks have seeped out from the love within the community. It's an odd feeling, to learn the legacy of a town from the buildings.

Clatter, chunk, chunk, clatter. The car slides off the even dirt road into a little winding path that meanders around a frozen field and disappears from sight. My father drives slowly, my mother tells him *Go straight*, and any moment I am expecting a tsunami of nausea to rear and collapse and shatter on my head. But the windows are open now, and the sounds of the dogs barking merrily are chimes of giddy fun as the Jeep jolts and swerves like bumper cars in an amusement park.

We're here, my mother announces, and we get off. The snow has been blown off the dirt path but it is frozen solid, and no dust cloud rises to greet our lonely steps. I reach out my hand to touch the grey cement walling the path, letting my fingers trail against the cool length, until we turn the corner- and then I realize that the wall was part of a house.

The green paint is peeling off the door, and I think faintly that it must have been a pretty door when it was first painted. My mother knocks, waits, then she knocks again, tries the door, anxiously waiting for response. None comes.

More knocking, and my mother blows on her red hands. *Perhaps he went out?*

Nonsense, my father says, and he points through the slim windows on the door. *The house is locked from the inside.* My mother's slender face lights up at this, and she moves to the side and taps the window instead. *Grandfather*, she calls in her pretty Mandarin Chinese. *Grandfather, would you open the door?*

What? I ask, and my mother comes back, rubbing her cold hands together. *That's his bedroom*, she tells me. *He must have been lying down.* The door creaks open then, and an old man with tufts of white hair and bleary membrane where an eye should be, greets us with a toothless smile. *Hello, hello!* He says.

This is my husband, and this is my daughter, my mother says clearly. My father steps forward and grasps his hands first, greeting him warmly, and then it's my turn. I shyly greet him as I clasp his hands, and I can feel the weathered skin, the knobbly fingers that have lost their joints and now become smooth rounded stumps.

Something about our gestures has pleased the grandfather, and he gives us an endearing toothless smile again as he ushers us inside. The house is frigid from the cement walls that hold no heat and the last of the incense sticks burning in the far corner have long lost their tiny warmth. In the room to the right yellow dried corn husks litter the cement floor, and a dusty blue electric cart sits, dilapidated and waiting. *Cellar,* my mother murmurs. Oh.

Take a look at the room on the left, she hints, and in three quick strides I am already standing at its doorway. Right under the windows there is a wide pane, a thin, flat board of wood, on which are heaped blankets and cloths. It must be his bed. *He was lying down when we came,* my mother tells me, and I venture a shy question. *Aren't you cold?*

My father's hearty voice echoes my query and the grandfather shakes his head. His eye twinkles merrily and his smile is wide. *Not cold,* he says. *Look.* By the bed there is a kettle, and he lifts it up to show me the glowing coals in the pail underneath it. Then the kettle must be hot, I think. And the handle is just plain iron- no rubber grip. The connections flash through my head as he puts the kettle back down, and when he straightens again I see a thick red band on his weathered palm. Is it a burn, or is it just the weight of the kettle? I pray it is the weight and not the burn. Rapidly my thoughts travel back to a story my sixth-grade teacher told me. The guttural staccato of my parents' Mandarin Chinese is quickly drowned out by the memory of a gentle but vivid Philippine voice.

"I was playing with my friends··· and then suddenly we saw this man walking down the street. He scratched his ear, just scratch, scratch, and we started laughing. And then suddenly- the ear comes off. We froze. He's standing there, looking at us, with this completely miserable, helpless look on his face, and then he looks at the ear in his hand, and then back at us."

"What did you do?"

"Me? I ran. I screamed and I ran."

Slowly the Mandarin Chinese engulfs me again in its bright hard tone and I come back to the present, to that bright toothless smile holding the wisdom and the pain of the ages. A mute part of my heart, still caught in the horror of the past, silently shrieks, don't let that happen here. Please, don't.

Should we go now, grandfather? My mother asks slowly, and he smiles as he lumbers over to the door again and out onto the grey dusty path. *He always comes with us to see the other grandfather, too,* she explains, and we follow him.

It does not take long to reach the other house, but there is chicken-coop wiring that comes amply to my shoulder, and at least five dogs are barking frantically at us by the time we have approached the doorbell. Two chickens study us with beady eyes. It's an adorable menagerie, I think, and I want to pet the dogs, but I fear they might bite. Just then a fur hat pokes out the door, and a tall, lean man with a lined, weathered face shambles outside.

Hello, grandfather! my mother calls, and her pretty Mandarin again rings through the air, quieting the dogs. The toothless grin next to me disappears under a torrent of words that are nearly indistinguishable due to the heavy accent, and the man in the fur hat responds likewise. Nudging a whimpering puppy out of the way with his foot, he opens the door fixed into the chicken-coop wiring and lets us in the yard.

As my father heartily grasps his hand I look at him, and then I look at him again. Search as I might, there seems to be nothing wrong. He smiles shyly under my curious gaze, and I hastily avert my eyes as he lifts a sleeve to wipe a furiously watering eye. Of course, I think; the beginning stages of leprosy. I hold out my hand but he has already crossed his arms, hiding his grimy hands from sight, and awkwardly I let my own drop.

But then everything about this man is a bit more quiet and a bit more awkward than it was at that frigid house of grey cement, and the grey sky and the grey earth press together against the grey trees heavily. I want to see his house, too, see how he has organized it, but he stands a few steps away from the door and warily keeps the rest of us standing at some distance.

Soon it is time to leave. Both men come trudging out to see us off, and we stand by the Jeep with the car doors swung open, urging both to hurry up and go on in. But they stay, stubbornly, wishing to see us on our way, and my mother whispers that they always like to see their visitors off. The warmth of the gesture moves my father beyond his normal courtesy for the elderly- for a man like my father it is harder to refrain from making a gesture of courtesy, than to make it, it has become so habitual- and he drives off with all the windows rolled down and our arms beating out a heartfelt good-bye and well-wishes to the two men. One has a wide toothless grin, the other has a small mustached smile, and both of them have their arms lifted in a similar salute.

A magpie alights on a branch, his startling black-and-white plumage fluttering in stark contrast against the dull monotone of neutral grey, and I look at it before I roll the windows up. It caws, *Come! Come!* And the silence rings, *Again! Again!*

When the car got back on the smoother dirt road my mom asked, *Well, how did you like it?*

I bounced up in my chair eagerly. *Can I play violin for them?*

My mom looked back to glance at me, and I remembered what she had said the last time. My face fell and she laughed at my forlorn expression. *I'm sure they'll appreciate the CD we're making, darling.*

It's not like I haven't thought of it, but the place is just too open…

There'll be another chance, kid, my father laughed, and he patted my hand comfortingly.

The touch of my father's warm hand on my cold one reminded me of the way the grandpa in the fur hat had crossed his arms. I was musing it over by myself when my mother asked me what I was thinking about.

Mom, why didn't the other man shake hands with me? He shook hands with Daddy.

My mother smiled. *He's been too used to having people shy away from him, darling. It's not because of you. But people generally don't want to touch them because they think leprosy is catching. He was actually being very considerate on his part.*

But all the same, be careful not to touch your mouth or your nose, my father said. *We'll stop by at that little shop and buy some water so that we can wash our hands.*

As I crouched down to wash my hands I couldn't help but feel the terrible irony. Just now I had been miserable because a grandfather wouldn't shake my hand- and he had done it out of consideration for me. And yet here I was, washing my hands as if I was trying to wash myself of a terrible impurity, as if I was trying to wash myself clean from blame and sin. Was I really different from any of the others, who didn't want to come near because they were scared of the risk of contaminating themselves? What was there to differentiate me? However practical and logical my actions might be, the truth remained that I saw both of them as people to be treated carefully, people I would need to beware.

And then suddenly it struck me that I was guilty of more than just shying away from the lepers, but also for the poor conditions in which they lived. There was another man's house that my mother had told me about, and promised to take me along to visit the next time. My mother worried that she would not be able to find it until she went a few more times with others who did know the way, since it was a little house hidden way off in the mountains. The leprosy had struck till the extent that the government was reluctant to let others see his malformed state. Thus he lived, like a prisoner in solitary confinement, with no company but his pipe and his phonograph and the yellow curtains that had become grey with the soot from the coal stove. The ventilation was terrible in that little house and there was no other place for the soot to escape but to the flat pieces of cloth tacked onto the windows during the winter. There had been several more people like him hounded into hiding by the government, but they had all died now, and only two people were continuing such hermit-like lives in the mountainous woods.

It wasn't like this state was worse than the other states, but then neither was it better. There were other counties, more to the south, where the government had actually relocated all the lepers to a separate town. The towns had terrible conditions, Auschwitzes and Dachaus of neglect. The government made no effort to make the towns particularly comfortable. This neglect was partly due to the belief that lepers were people struck by the heavens for their sins- a belief that was harder to root out than the belief in the Mandate of Heaven. Although they both originated from the very roots of China, the government had made a conscious effort to eradicate the belief about the Mandate; whereas about the former they only tried to keep the very existence of leprosy ignored and hidden, and pretend ignorance.

At least, in this county, there was no such town, but then neither were there even the meager funds that the lepers were supposed to be provided with- the government officials were not overly meticulous about allocating separate funds for the desperate, and most of them were willing to overlook a small miscalculation if it meant that a few more billfolds would be lining their wallets.

I could not help but feel guilty for this: feel guilty in lieu of the entire ignorant society, which for the most part was unconscious that such an atrocity was happening. Even had it directly witnessed the atrocity I doubt many would have stood up against it, due to that belief about leprosy being heaven's curse. But there was also another stronger guilt in me, that I was part of this very society, not only because I was bound to them but because I actually thought in ways similar to them. Again it was that fault in me that could not see these people as entities equal to myself. Had I not also shied away from them? The fundamental ugliness remained, and there was no way to rid myself of it.

My thoughts turned to a book I had re-read relatively recently-*Frankenstein*. The book is so famous today that most people will have probably read it at least once; if not the unabridged version, then at least the abridged version; and even in the case that they have not read either, they will still be relatively familiar with the name. Under the feverish hands and feverish mind of the Modern Prometheus a new race is created, a malformed terror created from the remnants of human corpses and galvanized by the human invention of electricity. A scientist's effort to make a new, beautiful race has resulted in the creation of a hideous monstrosity painful to behold.

The reason I thought of the book was because of an interesting question pertaining to the book, about the identity of the monster-a query that plagued Shelley since *Frankenstein's* first release. I first heard of it myself during Ms. Bell's AP Literature class not too long ago, when the seniors started studying the book. I was grading vocabulary quizzes just then but I kept an ear open as I checked the

Greek and Latin roots.

Ms. Bells asked the students who they thought of when they heard the name *Frankenstein*- the monster, or the scientist. Out of the sixteen students fifteen thought that Frankenstein referred to the monster. The misconception is an odd one, since in truth Shelley only calls the scientist Victor Frankenstein, Frankenstein; and all throughout the book the monster is merely referred to as "the monster" or "the wretch." The name does not change whether he is doing good or bad.

The reader, then, is left to question who Shelley really meant as the titular character, the protagonist, and who she meant to be the antagonist. What roles do the scientist and the monster play respectively in this Gothic horror story? Who is which? How are we to determine who is which?

Let us try to answer. The scientist, Victor Frankenstein, is the classically moody genius. He enjoys keeping to himself and brooding over deep thoughts, and when he finds something of interest he turns to it with a passion that is almost unearthly in his devotion to it. He is a fast learner and exceedingly ambitious. There are few lights that brighten up his morbid world of scientific obsessions, and those constitute his family, a few friends, and his love. He is not entirely unsympathetic, but his cold world of scientific thought and reasoning makes him as unapproachable as a calculator to most. If Victor is not a monster he is definitely something that is not entirely human.

What, then, about the nameless monster? He is a hideous brute of giant dimensions and unsettling features. The response he receives from society is necessarily one of repulsion and unwelcome- even his creator finds it difficult to tolerate being in the same room with him, so grotesque are his features. But that is truly judging, or rather misjudging, a book by its cover. Inside he is the sweetest being that could ever exist- a benevolent creature that would use his superhuman strength only to aid and save the lives of the endangered and the helpless. He longs for love and friendliness and hopes to find it somewhere, even though every society so far has repulsed him despite his actions of kindness.

But *Frankenstein* would be a fairly stagnant, as well as an unrealistic, tale if the story only focused on a munificent character willing to give endlessly to an unappreciative society. Instead the novel marks the spectacular demise of how characters become what the outside world makes them out to be. In short, the book is not of the life of a monster, but the process of the creation of a monster.

In the story of *Frankenstein*, the monster is driven to such extents of loneliness that he finally asks Victor Frankenstein to make him a female version of himself, one who would not loathe him for his despicable appearance. Frankenstein feels pity for this creature, his creation, but at the same time he cannot help but feel the revulsion that is shared by everyone else upon seeing the gruesome face of this creation. Frankenstein's refusal leads to a change of heart in the monster: having been betrayed by everyone, and with no more hope of circumstances ever changing for the better now that even his creator has deserted him, the monster curses his life and swears vengeance on Victor's life and happiness- the source of his own unhappy existence. It is from that moment on that the monster truly becomes a monster, a figure of fear that will shadow forever the life of Victor Frankenstein.

Where did the initial benevolence go? Wherever goodness goes when evil enters- out. And ironically, it was his very creator, Victor Frankenstein, that caused him to become thus; by refusing to come to terms with his own creation.

Yet this story does not rely solely on the relationship between the creator and the creation. If anything it relies more heavily on the relationship between the monster and the society. It must be noted that the monster made more approaches to people in the outside world than solely to his creator. If just one person in the society had opened their heart to him, then no monster would have appeared. As non-human as the monster may have looked, he would still have had the twin integral needs in humans, acceptance and love, fulfilled, and he would have become a fine contribution to society.

It was that insane loneliness and longing for acceptance that caused the monster to turn into what people feared him to be. And since the creator refused to create a society in which his creation could survive and be happy, the creation in turn destroyed the society of the creator.

It reminded me of the story my father told me as we drove back home that day. When my father was young there were lepers in his village, afflicted people who would traipse from street to street and house to house begging for alms and goods. Following Korean customs they would cling onto Korea housewives, calling them "sister" and "mother" and using every term of respectful endearment possible, to wring out food or money.

There was also a widespread rumor at the time that the tender heart of a young child would cure leprosy, and mothers generally clutched their babies and eyed the lepers with suspicion when they came near. It probably was a rumor started to keep the children away from the lepers, since children are more easily susceptible to the affliction than adults are. But the truth is that the children believed it, and so did the adults, and so did the lepers- which caused the biggest problem of all.

What happened was, when my father was very young, he had wandered out a good way from his home, when he was caught by lepers eager to try for a chance to be cured. My father redefined the meaning of the phrase "a narrow shave" that day. One of the lepers was grinding his knife when a man from my father's neighborhood walked by and happened to notice that something unusual was going on in the wheat field.

I shudder to imagine what would have happened, had not that neighbor walked by. It was a touch of divine intervention.

But are the lepers to blame? For them it was a disease that had plagued them for heaven knows how long. It was a barrier that would forever cause them to be shunned and despised by society. Who would not have paid an equal, if not dearer, price to be healed? If society had ever looked at them with a warmer heart, a welcome gaze, would they ever have been tempted to commit such an atrocity as to eat a child's heart, even if it they detested their affliction?

No one single person has the power to so completely demonize a character. The line between monster and scientist is faintly ingrained into any division, and beyond the division the line broadens into a much wider spectrum under which many categories fall. Thus as much as we would like to condemn a single character for the demise of a person, blame just one and get it over with, we learn that it is impossible to allocate all the blame specifically to that one person. The entire society is to blame.

From this point of view there is so much to learn from the people who live in the same towns as the lepers do, the ones that are willing to open up their arms and their hearts where the rest of us cannot. Not too long ago we drove to the same little town and the road had, by then, sufficiently melted to send up dust clouds whenever we- or the car- moved. When we parked the car, with the last of a dust cloud swirling around and settling on the rear, I noticed a woman watching us, her shovel facing down as her keen eyes busily followed the minute revolutions of the wheels. I don't know clearly if we disturbed her work, but it definitely seemed as if she had been working, and the dust cloud that bloomed from the car tracks had stopped her.

In a way she reminded me of Jean-Francois Millet's *The Gleaners*, the art piece famous for having endowed its farmers with a simple but dignified humility. Any moment she would start working again, and then when the time came perhaps she would look up shyly at the sky and give thanks, but as she worked her eyes would look out at the world with the wisdom and the kind patience of the ages living in the gaze of her eyes.

We stepped out of the car and her keen eyes and her weathered face looked out at us silently. Instinctively and impulsively I bowed my head lightly, shyly greeting her with a softly murmured Chinese phrase. A flash of welcome and goodwill lit up her face as she smiled back at me.

It was surprising, I later confided to my mother, how that smile changed her face so completely. The difference was that of a jack-o-lantern at night-time without and with a candle. My mother was not surprised.

They're living with the lepers, and that requires a lot more courage and openness than what you can find in most communities, she said. *There's another town that when a new car comes in the entire community gathers together to see who it is, and then when you leave they all see you off at once. Maybe some of it's because a town's still a town, not like a city. But a larger part of it is because everyone here is willing to accept more. They're willing to give up more. It's a real community.*

I thought awhile over that. All in all it was just so Frankensteinish that I felt sorry, but yet there was elation in me, too- elation that this story, at least, would end differently. Here there were no disappointed Frankensteins shunned by the world. Here there was a world that was open and loving and accepting, and there was a slot where every individual could fit into, as components of a giant and complex jigsaw puzzle.

But out there, there were different worlds where no one accepted the lepers, sometimes worlds where no one knew they existed. I hung my head in shame again. When I had first visited the lepers

I had wanted to play violin for them, but my parents had told me it was out of the question- for reasons that seemed completely unjustifiable, I had thought petulantly. The Chinese government was ashamed of its lepers and wanted only to hide their existence, and our playing music for them would be tantamount to advertising their existence. We wouldn't have been allowed to go and visit them anymore. The most we could do as of now was to fundraise, and to visit them and grasp their hands to remind them that some people in the outside world knew they existed and were trying to work for them.

It's horrendous, I said to myself, while I thought, it's the Frankensteins of today.

We traveled awhile in silence, and then we crossed under a bridge that we had laughed over on the way going. The bridge crossed not too high over the highway, and I suppose something must have gone wrong since it was under construction. A section of a bridge was supported with red metal lifts and steel wire and white plastic boards, and right above the third lane of the going cars, a large block of cement and tar hung precariously over the highway road. A red crane, swinging high above the bridge, helped the block, but not by much, since the cranes and the bridge had both been discarded and the workers were taking their weekend off.

My father clicked his tongue disapprovingly. *This is the only country that I can imagine would let a bridge remain in such a dangerous position*, he said, a frown slashing his forehead. *The danger to the people passing under- its very own people-*

And my mother and I both heard the unsaid criticism as clearly as if he had said it out loud, in the silence that followed. How much weaker China made her weakest. How more vulnerable China made her most vulnerable. All of us were at the mercy of a swinging mass of cement and tar that might come crashing down on any car, but at least we had the choice to pass under that bridge or not. The weak and the vulnerable have no choices; they must simply follow.

The rest of the drive passed in broken pieces of silence that slid together in smooth planes with the rest of the shards of reveries and murmurs.

*****

Hurry up, darling, my mother calls, and I dash into the car. As we speed along again, munching this time on cookies and coffee, I realize that the nausea and the fear of the first trip has now come to recede into only a faintly palpable tinge of dizziness that makes me lie down near the end of the trip, and with candy even the dizziness disappears completely.

The birds sing delightfully today and today the entire world is a chromatic harmony. The colors are crisp and new, as if they have been washed and aired and freshly ironed, and spring whispers in every breath of the wind. I recall the grey of the last visit and I cannot help but chuckle at the memory of winter. Winter is a desolate thing when it is far away but when it is near or present it is an adorable thing of perverse warmth. Just now it has been a little too long present to be quite adorable, but with the new touches of color stealing into the world the grey warmth has again relocated itself in my world of likes.

The road flies by easily and we slide right off the tar into the dusty brown of the country road, tumbling into the brown dust that flies in specks and clouds as we rev the engine. The world is crisper and brighter out here. I like it.

Again we walk by the grey cement walls, but they are the only things that have remained grey. As we round the corner we see the toothless grandfather working on a little stool, fixing something. The brown fields have already been planted with little green baby shoots.

Hello, hello! He cries, and his merry cry rings out heartily and echoes in our own greetings. He proudly leads us inside to see the blue electric cart, dragged out right in front of the door. It is shiny and polished. The grandfather must have been fixing the seat, since the black leather of the seat has disappeared. To the side, in a large stone pan, there are two large buns. *Breakfast*, he tells us, and his eye crinkles into a smile. I hardly notice that he has lost one eye anymore, since through that one eye he speaks of more charm and delight and friendliness than most people can with two.

A while later we amble over, all together, to the lean man's house, and one of the dogs comes and nuzzles my hand through the wire. It is a little black darling that has a slight limp in its left forepaw and bright dark eyes sparkling with naughtiness. The lean man smiles as he sees the dog paw at my jeans. He moves as if to nudge it away with his foot, but I smile at him and draw the dog a little closer to me instead. When I get up I shake his hand, warmly, and he doesn't try to hide his hand from me anymore, whether it's because he knows I don't care if it's grimy, or whether it's because he knows that I want nothing more than to give him as much warmth as I can give, if it is only through touching hands.

Again the clamor of hands and whoosh of color as the car leaves the little town behind, and we are back on the road, flying back towards the city and away from the kindness of the people who love and who are loved.

But again on the highway we slow down as we see against the blue sky and the greening hills, the grey slab of cement swinging from the bridge. It's a precarious position, even more so than last time, and I fear that someday soon the bridge will come trembling down and crash upon the passing cars. It's been like that for over two months now, and we have concluded that the bridge will just stay so until the end of time, a slab that will initiate Armageddon.

But the frozen red crane supporting the slab swings up, creaks, and inches the slab slightly up- though we pass by, smoothly, swiftly, and safely, into a different world where the Frankensteins are still the monsters.

Works Referenced

Plays

Ibsen, Henrik. A Doll's House. Project Gutenberg,
2002. Web. 10 Dec. 2013

Ibsen, Henrik. Hedda Gabler. Project Gutenberg,
2013. Web. 10 Dec. 2013

Shakespeare, William. Three Tragedies. New York: Penguin Books,
1970. Print.

Shaw, George Bernard. Pygmalion. New York: Penguin, 2000. Print.

Shaw, George Bernard. Mrs. Warren's Profession. Project Gutenberg,
2012. Web. 10 Dec. 2013

Wilde, Oscar. The Importance of Being Earnest. Project Gutenberg,
2006. Web. 10 Dec. 2013

Wilde, Oscar. Lady Windermere's Fan. Project Gutenberg,
2002. Web. 10 Dec. 2013

Wilde, Oscar. A Woman of No Importance. Project Gutenberg,
1997. Web. 10 Dec. 2013

Wilde, Oscar. An Ideal Husband. Project Gutenberg,
2009. Web. 10 Dec. 2013

Williams, Tennessee. Cat on a Hot Tin Roof. New York: University of
the South, 2004. Print.

Williams, Tennessee. A Streetcar Named Desire. New York: University
of the South, 2004. Print.

Williams, Tennessee. The Glass Menagerie. New York: University of the
South, 2011. Print.

Novels

Carroll, Lewis. Alice's Adventures in Wonderland and Through the Looking-Glass. London: Wordsworth, 2001. Print.

Faulkner, William. A Rose for Emily. Logan: Perfection Learning Corporation, 2007. Print.

Fitzgerald, Scott. Tender is the Night. Planet eBook, 1933. Web. 10 Dec. 2013

Fitzgerald, Scott.The Great Gatsby. London: Wordsworth, 1993. Print.

Hurston, Zora Neale. Their Eyes Were Watching God. New York: HarperCollins, 2009. Print.

Mitchell, Margaret. Gone With the Wind. New York: Pocket Book, 1996. Print.

Morrison, Toni. Beloved. New York: Penguin, 1988. Print.

Rand, Ayn. Atlas Shrugged. New York: Penguin, 1994. Print.

Rand, Ayn. The Fountainhead. New York: Penguin, 1994. Print.

Shelley, Mary. Frankenstein. New York: Bantam Classics, 1981. Print.

Steinbeck, John. The Pearl. New York: Penguin, 1992. Print.

Twain, Mark. The Adventures of Huckleberry Finn. New York: Scholastic, 1987. Print.

Wharton, Edith. "Roman Fever." Classic Short Stories. Ed. Rosemary Gray. New York: Wordsworth, 2007. Print.

Wharton, Edith. The Age of Innocence. London: Wordsworth, 1999. Print.